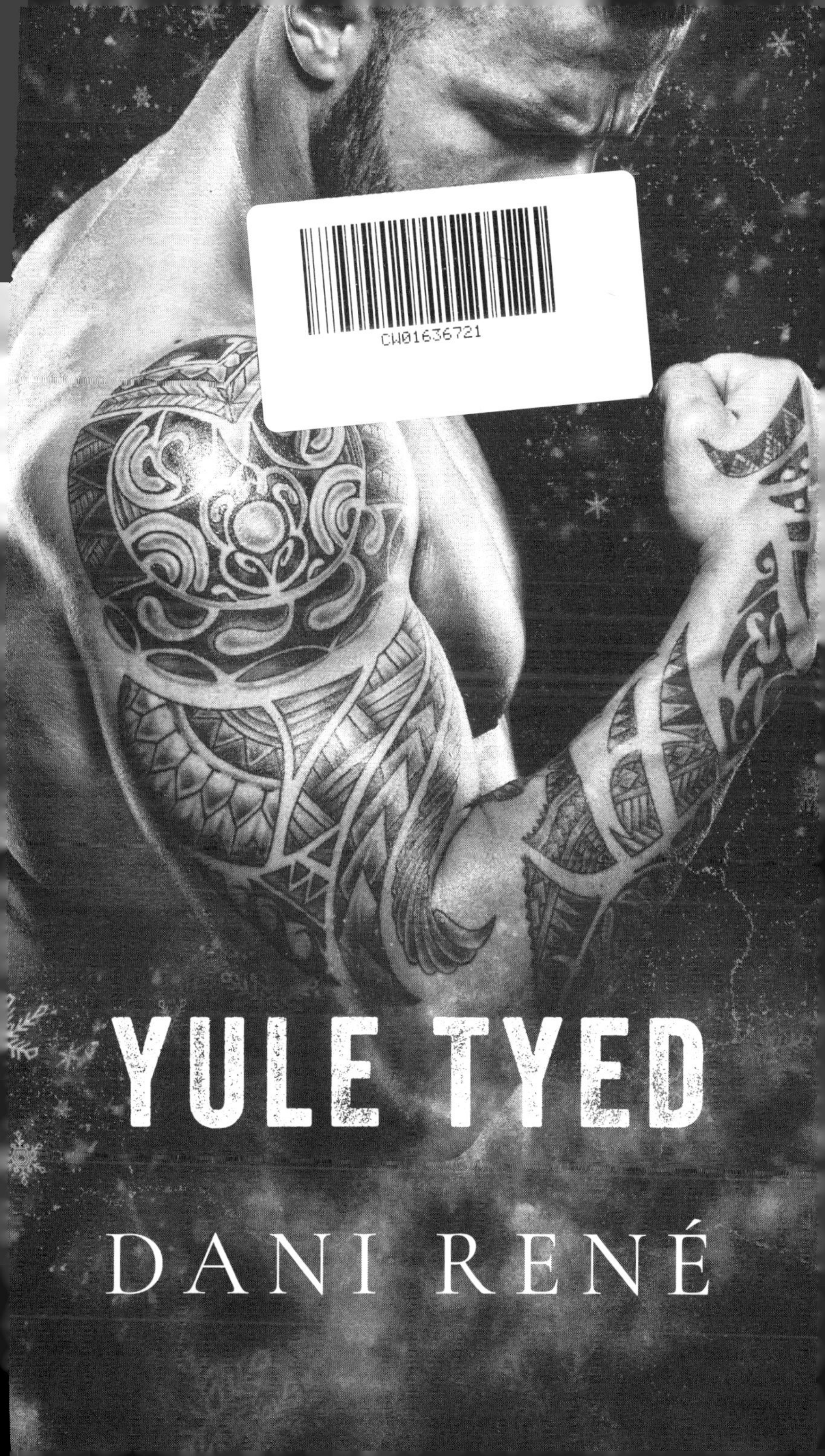
YULE TYED
DANI RENÉ

Edited by Emily Lawrence
Proofread by Sheena Taylor

Print ISBN: 978-1-8381794-9-6

Cover Design & Formatting by Raven Designs

AUTHOR'S NOTE

Dear Reader,

Please note, this is written in British English, with Irish slang, so some words may be spelled differently than what you're used to. It is a work of fiction, and some details may have been embellished slightly.

Now, you're welcome to dive in and spend Christmas with the Royal Bastards.

Mad love,
Dani, xo

ROYAL BASTARDS MC

BELFAST, NORTHERN IRELAND

A broken heart
Laid in wait
It's stolen love
Kidnapped in haste

Memories sting
Of a magic kiss
A tender touch
Etched in bliss

Moons had past
Inside I burned
Into my arms
She would return

Our endless bond
Time could not fade
It grew in strength
As if she stayed

Ablaze
_hydrus

More from Hydrus at

www.hydruspoetry.com

ROYAL BASTARDS CODE

PROTECT: The club and your brothers come before anything else, and must be protected at all costs. CLUB is FAMILY.

RESPECT: Earn it & Give it. Respect club law. Respect the patch. Respect your brothers. Disrespect a member and there will be hell to pay.

HONOR: Being patched in is an honor, not a right. Your colors are sacred, not to be left alone, and NEVER let them touch the ground.

OL' LADIES: Never disrespect a member's or brother's Ol'Lady. PERIOD.

CHURCH is MANDATORY.

LOYALTY: Takes precedence over all, including well-being.

HONESTY: Never LIE, CHEAT, or STEAL from another member or the club.

TERRITORY: You are to respect your brother's property and follow their Chapter's club rules.

TRUST: Years to earn it…seconds to lose it.

NEVER RIDE OFF: Brothers do not abandon their family.

PLAYLIST

Fairy Tale of New York - The Pogues

Missing You - Christy Moore

It's My Life - Bon Jovi

With Arms Wide Open - Creed

Everything You Want - Vertical Horizon

All I Want For Christmas Is You - Mariah Carey

Find the full playlist on Spotify

PROLOGUE

Tye

Seventeen Years Old

The sun sets on another short, autumn day in Ballycastle. The sky has darkened already when I make my way down to the beach. Livin' this far north of Belfast has its perks. I've grown up in the small town, and I know everyone. But that's where its drawbacks seem to come alive as well.

My da is a shopkeeper in the high street, and if I fuck up, he hears about it from the gossipin' ol' biddies who spy from their lounge windows. When we pass by, we can see the curtains shift ever so slightly. I'm a bit of a troublemaker when it comes down to it. But Da can be thankful I don't do drugs and shite like that.

"Tye," the soft voice of my best friend calls my name as she nears me.

Einin has been in my life for so long, since I was a wee one, and I've never known a world without her. Those eyes, golden and shimmerin', always looked at me as if I were her hero. And while I wanted to be, I don't believe I'm good enough for her.

We're all meant to be deciding what we want to do with our lives, but we're not even out of our feckin' teens yet. She smiles, and it's as if the world spins on its axis. When I turned sixteen, I started noticin' her more. I knew I shouldn't because we were mates. But I couldn't help it. As she blossomed, somethin' inside me clicked.

"Are ye ready for this?" I ask her as I take her hand. It's not the first time we've come out here, but it's the last time we will for a wee while.

"Aye." She nods while liftin' her chin in defiance.

One thing about my wee bird is that she's strong. Her personality shines through in her soulful expression. It makes me smile whenever I look at her. When there's somethin' dangerous to do, she's always the first to step up and take the risk.

I lead her out onto the basalt. Legend has it that Finn McCool, a giant who lived here eons ago, created them. I'd rather believe that, than accept they were merely the result of volcanic eruptions. Einin giggles when we reach the water as we watch the small waves hit the black rock.

Reachin' into my pocket, I pull out my pocketknife and flick the blade.

"Do ye think Finn would be angry at us doing this?" Einin asks me, innocent intrigue clear in her voice.

"Naw." I shake my head and grin down at her. "He'll think we're all right," I tell her. "You'll be safe with me." My words make her smile—a wide, cheerful grin that lightens her expression and makes her eyes sparkle like gold in the sunlight.

This far north, the weather can be unpredictable, but today, it's been grand. I drop to a crouch. Einin follows suit and settles beside me. The gentle breeze along the ocean wafts her perfume into my nostrils. Takin' a deep inhale, I smile as I start carvin' into the rock. Perhaps we shouldn't deface the stone, but many have done it, and deep down, I want proof that Einin existed in my life.

"I can't believe I have to go," she tells me then. It has been a sore subject since I first found out her ma was sendin' her away. "And just before the fair."

I glance over my shoulder at her. Those pink lips purse into a pout, and I'm tempted to lean in and kiss her. I've wanted to for a couple of years now, but I've always bottled it. The fear of her rejectin' me in *that* way has kept me at a distance. My feelings, at least.

"I want you to stay," I tell her before turnin' to finish up etchin' my name and then hers in the rock. The black basalt will forever hold our names. At least until the water eats away at it. But I'm pretty sure it will be a few hundred years before that happens. We'll both be long gone.

"Aye, but ye know Ma is not going ta listen ta me. Even though I can finish my final year at school in Antrim. Da has poisoned her mind against the school here, and now she's on about it being shite." She shakes her head, her gaze lookin' out over the water, and she focuses on the horizon, but I can't take my eyes off her.

Einin's Da lives in London, in some posh house with a maid and a swimmin' pool. Even though I know it's for the best, for her education, I can't help but have the anger simmerin' deep in my gut. No matter which school she goes to, she'll excel, but he's convinced she needs to be in the Big Smoke.

We stare at our names. Einin's hand slides against mine, and our fingers tangle. Havin' a friend like her has been a challenge over the past few weeks, but I know if I don't take a chance now, I'm goin'ta regret it all my life.

Slowly, I turn to face her before releasin' her hand and cuppin' her face. There are tears shinin' in her eyes. The moment she blinks, they'll trickle down her cheeks, much like the day I overheard her ma tellin' her she's leavin'. Einin didn't know I was standin' at the door, and I ended up walkin' away. When I should have stayed, held her.

"I made a mistake," I tell her. "I should have never left you with her that day."

"It wasn't yer fault," she insists, the same way she's done for the past week since we both realised she'll not be here for the new school year.

I sigh, knowin' I'm about to complicate things. But I do it anyway. Leanin' in, I place my lips on hers. I don't know if she's in shock at me kissin' her, or if she's reciprocatin', but she doesn't push me away. Her lips part, and I take it as an invitation.

Suddenly, her arms are around my neck, twinin' tightly, and I allow my hands to trail down to her arse.

Grippin' her, I lift her against me. She's so slight. My body cocoons hers as I hold on to her.

When I pull away, we're both pantin'. Her eyes glazed over and her pupils dilated. My hands are still holdin' on to her arse, and it feels perfect to have her against me. Einin fits me. There's no other way about it. She's mine. She was made to be mine.

"I…" Her lips are swollen, wet, allurin'. I want to capture them again. But I don't. Before I can say anything, she whispers, "We shouldn't have done that. It's going to ruin every—"

"It's not ruined anythin'," I tell her while shakin' my head. "We needed to know."

"Know what?" Even though she seems worried, she doesn't let go of me, and I don't release her. I don't want to, ever. But I know the moment we get back into town, she's goin' to have to leave. She'll walk away, and I won't see her again for at least a year.

"Promise me ye'll write to me," I say, ignorin' the question she posed. "I need to know ye're okay, wee bird." The need to protect her runs through my veins. I'm pretty sure it always will.

My request makes her smile. "Aye," she whispers before pressin' her lips to mine, briefly. "I promise ye, big man," she teases, usin' the nickname she gave me one night.

When I asked her why the name, she explained that when we first met at nine years old. I was so much taller than her. And she was convinced I was all grown up. Einin admitted she'd called me that in her head ever since.

"Good." I pull her to her feet and take her hand. That went better than I expected. At least she didn't smack me for kissin' her. But with every step closer to my bike, the agony in my stomach churns.

She's goin' ta walk away, and there's nothin' I can do about it.

CHAPTER ONE

Tye

A broken heart is as bad as bein' gutted while awake.

There are no fairy tales in my world.

On my sixteenth birthday, I said goodbye to my best friend. I watched her walk away, and I let her because I was stuck in a small town with no options but to finish school.

As much as I wanted to follow, I knew I couldn't. There was never a choice in the matter. She was goin' to leave, anyway. There were better things out there for her, and I knew it. She couldn't stay in Ballycastle. As beautiful as the town is, there's not much opportunity for a free spirit. So, instead of tellin' her the one thing I knew I should have, I kept my mouth shut, and I focused on followin' in Da's footsteps. It's stupid when I think about it now.

But the name on the computer screen takes me back to that day. Since then, till now, seven years later, she still makes me want more. When I turned away from the bus pullin' out of town, I knew I would never be the same. And even though I worked for Da until he sold the shop, I was never happy again.

I left the small town I grew up in and made my way to the big city. Da had given me some of his savings to find a new life. I studied and found my love for computers instead. When I'm focused on the coding, the inner workings of how networks and websites are run, and how they're secured by secret algorithms, I forget.

I joined the Royal Bastards because of that. It's not somethin' my father would have wanted for me, but I've found a family I never thought I would have. It was always Da and me. Now I have brothers who will do anythin' for me.

Panic sets in the moment I hack into the email trail. What I'm findin' isn't just a missin' person, or the head of the Irish mob. It is so much bigger. Puzzle pieces slam together, crashin' as they make up the image that's formin' in my mind.

Pushin' up from my chair, I make my way into the lounge where the guys are sittin'. Rebel is the first to look at me, the worry clear in his eyes. He's thinkin' about Callia. We're all concerned about her, but what I found may be a windfall, and we have to act fast because time is against us.

"Lads, I think you need to see this," I say from the entrance to the livin' room. The three of them turn to look at me, and their focus is now locked.

"What is it?" Monster says as he rises before headin' my way.

If it weren't for him, I'm not sure where I would be. After years of having the quiet of a small town to surround me, when I arrived in Belfast, there were too many distractions. Even though I graduated, I still had a lot of growin' up to do. Monster put my mind to work, he welcomed my skills, and I never left.

"Follow me." I turn and make my way into the office with all three men right behind.

Settlin' into the chair at my desk, I pull up the files. The screen fills with profiles on all the criminals who are on the most wanted lists across the world, includin'

Bragan.

"What are we looking at, Tye?" Sully leans in, his head beside mine as he scans the images on the screen.

"Each of these are men who are suspects in a traffickin' ring." I open the one they'll recognise first. Patrick Bragan. The man who took Callia? Or more like convinced her he was her father. Rebel's hiss from behind me tells me he's not happy. His girl is gone. Even though he and Callia weren't officially together, there was no doubt he cared about her. "It seems there are links between Bragan and the Bratva, but it's not lookin' good because this goes all the way to America, Asia, even down to New Zealand, where Sinéad Bragan was headed before we intercepted her." Sinéad, Patrick's wife, was arrested only a couple of weeks ago and is done for. Somethin' tells me she's not gettin' released any time soon. Now that Scotland Yard and MI5 have her, she's goin' to be put away for a very long time.

"Volkov," Monster murmurs. "I've heard that name whispered for years. Da may have even mentioned him. Do you think this goes back to my father?"

Shruggin', I open Volkov's profile. "All they have on him are his organisation links, which are pretty much all over the world. He even has ties to the Italians. I'm not sure if ye can get Venier on it?" I glance over my shoulder to look at Monster who is in contact with the soon to be Boss of the mafia family.

"Aye," he says with a nod.

"There's another name that has come up repeatedly," I explain. "Malcolm Savage. Not sure what happened, but he hasn't been active in years. It was after Malcolm disappeared that Volkov started recruiting men of power. He knows he can get women and girls through these criminal organisations. But there has been a run-in with an American he hired, a man called Mahoney, who ran riot through the States."

As I scroll through the pages, clickin' on each one, Monster, Sully, and Rebel read through the details. This sick bastard preyed on children. It makes my stomach churn when I think about what he's done.

"They still have active members who find new girls every few months. There's a pattern." Rebel points to the screen where each date is confirmed and co-ordinated perfectly in time with major holidays.

Monster leans in, takin' a closer look. There are still questions I haven't been able to pinpoint answers for, but what I have figured out is these men are intelligent, calculated. "Looks like they run their auctions every six months."

"Aye," I say as I open the email trail once more. "It keeps them under the radar. Every auction has been kept secret until the day it takes place, which means it's difficult for the peelers to track them down."

"Find out all you can," Monster tells me. "We'll meet in a couple of hours. Bring the info to church, and we'll plan the best way to do this. I don't want anyone gettin' hurt."

"Will do."

I focus on the computer spewin' out names to me, and as I delve deeper into the web, I find more and more missin' girls. I'm not sure how long I sit in the office, but Miren has brought me somethin' to eat, and yet, I haven't moved.

When I open a new browser and get a search runnin', my software beeps to alert me somethin' has come up. I glance at the second screen to find a new auction that's goin'ta be runnin' on Christmas day.

These feckers have no morals. They're only focused on the money they make and the lives they destroy. Pullin' up one email, I note the information that will take us to France. Monster has contacts that can get us there in a few hours, which means we can get ahead of them.

Openin' the attachments on the email, I find the

first one a photo of a girl. Each file has been labelled with a number, which I'm guessin' is how they identify the captives. They don't use names, these captives are merely stock to them. Nothin' more.

I open the next, and the next. Each one printin' out from beside my computer. We can take these to Scotland Yard, who can then inform the French law enforcement agencies. Assumin' they're not in these bastard's pockets.

When I open the fifth photo, my world tilts on its axis. The room spins, and my ears ring with loud thuds of my pulse. Starin' back at me is my past. Those familiar eyes are drained of life. There's no longer a sparkle in her stare.

As her photo prints, I realise there's no time to sit back and wait. We have to act fast. And I'm goin'ta be front and centre for this.

Pickin' up the printout, I rush from the office, almost slammin' into Monster, who's makin' his way to his office. He looks at me, and I can tell from the expression of concern I must look like I've seen a ghost.

I have.

"We need to get to France now."

"What are ye talkin' about?"

I shove the photo at him before sayin', "She's in

danger. They all are, but she's..." My words are stuck in my throat, threatenin' to suffocate me.

"Who is this?" Monster glances at the photo then up at me. "Ye know her?"

"Aye," I choke out. "She... we were best friends as kids." My chest tightens when I think about her in danger. When I consider what she may already have been through, my hands fist at my sides. "We have to go find her. I have to be there fer her."

"Okay," Monster says with a nod. "But we will plan this out. I'll call the brothers in now, and we'll get the details cleared up."

He's right. I know he is, but I'm tense. My shoulders are tight, achin' with the need to rush out of this house right now.

"I can't let her get sold."

"We won't," Monster assures me. "Family stick together."

By the time we're in church, I'm on the edge of my feckin' seat.

"This is time-sensitive," Monster says to the men. "I want two of you to stay back, to keep the women here safe. But the rest of us will fly out. I've spoken with Judah. The Venier jet is ours to use if we need it. It will be the easiest and quickest way to get there. We'll also be able to take a handful of bikes and pick up a hired SUV when we land."

"I say we fly out tonight. The sooner we get there, the more time we have to suss out the property. We'll have an edge, and they won't know what hit them." Sully's voice booms as he slams his fist on the smooth surface of the table.

I knew they wouldn't let me down. We are family. We have each other's backs. And I know that no matter what happens from here on out, we will save those girls.

I will save Einin.

CHAPTER TWO

Einin

I slip on the shorts that hug my bum. They're like a second skin and don't hide the fact I'm not wearing any knickers. With the top that cups my breasts, it's a matching set of perfectly sculpted underwear. I may as well be wearing nothing at all. They could have painted parts of my body, and I'd feel less exposed.

My body has transformed over the years. But the sadness that has kept a hold of me all this time is still there, ever present. I've become accustomed to ignoring it. Where I focus rather on the numbness than the emotion. As we head into the end of another year where my life is nothing more than a reminder of being taken, used, trained, I wonder if it's time to stop fighting for my freedom.

It's almost Christmas, and I think back to my sixteenth birthday. I was born on the twenty-third of December, and Ma always told me it's because I was special. It was the most magical time of the year, which is why I have never forgotten the moment I noticed Tye in a different light.

"Tye." I smile when I open the door.

We've decorated the house with balloons, ribbons, and an enormous banner that says, 'Happy Birthday'. My best friend is here, but the dreams I've been having changed the way I look at him now. Since I've known him, he's focused on working out, but more now that he's already turned seventeen. The girls notice him, stare his way when we walk past, but the thing is, he's never had a girlfriend.

"Happy birthday, wee bird," he teases with a smile that makes my heart thrum faster than I thought it could. I wonder if he can hear it because it's deafening to me. He's nicknamed me 'wee bird' because my name literally means 'little bird' *and that's always what Tye has called me. Nobody else could use that name.*

Ma reckons we'll get married someday, but I have a

feeling she's got those heart eyes. She wants me to be happy, to have something she never did. As much as I love her, I feel as if I'm not good enough for Tye. He has a good heart, he's strong, handsome, and he would make any lass happy. But I'm pretty sure he sees me as a friend. Nothing more.

I haven't told him how I feel. It's something my diary has kept secret since I wrote about it months ago. He's never even kissed me. And it's the only thing I can think about every time I'm near him.

"I'm not wee anymore, Tye," I tell him, a giggle escaping my lips and he offers me the grin I love.

Aye, I've loved him for a long time, but now, it's not only as a friend, he's so much more. He's my rock. He knows me better than anyone else, better than I know myself. And I still don't know why he wants to be friends with me.

I've never been part of the popular crowd. My focus was on school. I wanted to go to University and make Ma proud. And with my grades, I'm pretty sure I'll get there on a bursary. The financial aid will help because I know Ma doesn't have the money to pay for my living expenses, or the course I want to do. And taking out a loan is not an option either.

"Ye'll always be my wee bird," he tells me and pulls me into his muscular arms. The older he gets, the more muscle he builds, and the stronger he is. But the tighter he holds me,

the safer I feel. And I realise I never want him to let me go.

Tye's affection made me feel as if I were snuggled at home, like nothing could ever hurt me when he was close by. The difference between Tye and the man who now owns me is that there is always a false sense of security in the promise in my captor's eyes. Not only him, though, but all the traffickers who buy and sell girls and young women.

The rooms we're given, the clothes, and the luxuries. Gold painted shit may hide the filth, but there's a stench of evil. With each gift of beauty comes a stark reminder of darkness, of the violence that runs through their veins.

It's been years since they first sold me from one home to another, and it's happened twice a year since. I've watched girls come and go. Some even stayed. Only a handful, though. These men aren't in the habit of keeping pets around for long, because this isn't some posh life that makes us feel special. They ensure we know we're not. We are toys, drones who follow orders or we face the consequences.

But this place I'm in now, I've only been here for a few months. And yet, I feel more at ease here than any of the other houses I've been sent to. I've overheard whispers we're in France. The weather has been chilly, even with the sunny days, and they allow us into the garden, which I've taken advantage of more times than I can count.

I glance in the mirror and shudder. I look nothing like the girl who packed her bags and left Northern Ireland seven years ago. My thoughts have strayed to home, to Ballycastle so many times. The green hills, the ocean, and the boy I left behind.

I promised him I'd write every single day for that year. He was stuck at school, but I couldn't. I didn't even make it to school. They brought in tutors to make sure we didn't fall behind. The men who bought us wanted to ensure we were intelligent because it made them look good if we were able to hold a conversation with their friends and confidantes about any subject possible. It was the only thing I was thankful for. I graduated, but I still don't see the light at the end of the tunnel.

Missy walks into the room, stopping short at the entrance. She's been here longer than I have. She once told me she arrived here at a much younger age. The man who purchased her from the auction is good to her. I'm pretty sure she's in love with him. He is handsome, I can't deny it, but he is dangerous. She told me he's French royalty, or something like that. But I haven't been here long enough to know if it's true. The one thing I know is, he's prone to violence. Even though he's never struck one of us, he's still issued threats that force us to obey.

"The party is about to start," she tells me. "The guests are all in the living room." Her American accent is a gentle reminder that the girls who come to these *parties,* as the men call it, are from all over the world. It's not just one targeted country.

"Do I look okay?" I turn to her, waiting for her to assess the outfit. We've become close friends, and I'm thankful for that.

The home I was in before coming here was hell. They kept us in our rooms twenty-four seven, and even then, we were bound. There was enough leeway to move to the bathroom if we needed it, but we could never leave.

Missy comes to me and offers a smile. "You're beautiful," she tells me. It's something we remind each other of daily.

When you're here, as a possession, it's not the same as having a normal life. We're constantly told we're nothing more than pets.

"Are the boys coming too?" I ask, curious to see her reaction.

A blush creeps up onto her cheeks at the mention of

the twins, and she smiles. "Yes."

The twins—who arrived at the same time as Missy—are confident, handsome, and they only have eyes for her. Since she and I have grown close, they've accepted me as part of their friendship circle.

"Good," I say with a nod. I feel better when we're all together.

Even though these men outnumber us, there's a sense of security having my friends there. We hold hands as we make our way out of my room and down the hall. The house is old, enormous, with countless rooms. Expensive art hangs on the walls, mostly portraits of people from centuries ago. The smooth wooden floors have been varnished to shine, while the accents of gold and copper shimmer. Plants flourish the interior, offering a homely feel to the house, and from every window, there's a view of lush green hills. It's almost like being in paradise, but under the beautiful veneer, it's nothing more than a gilded prison.

"There they are," one twin, Josh, says.

The other twin, Jacques, walks up to us and smiles. I learnt early on that his name is James, but because our owner prefers his pets to have alternative names for their new lives, he changed it to something more fitting with where they are now. He gave Josh the name

Josué, but he never uses it. He refuses to be anything other than Josh to us.

"Are we ready?" A deep French accent comes from the threshold to the lounge.

The butler, who we only know as Louis, steps up to us with the four leashes and collars in hand. He first collars the lads, then, he comes towards me. Lifting my hair, I wait for the soft leather to encircle my neck.

Missy is last, and then, we're led like dogs into a room where we find the men who have been here repeatedly over the few months since I arrived. All of them are dressed in their best tailored suits. Some in black and others in navy blue, all with crisp white shirts and ties that pop against the stark colours of their jackets.

Andre Laurent, our owner, smiles when he sees us. Our black outfits—that barely cover anything at all—clearly please him. The butler takes us to him. Without a word, Louis hands over the leashes and leaves us with the men.

I'm not sure what celebration it is tonight. It's nearing Christmas, which is in a few days. I used to love the festive season, but it's become something of a nightmare, and I no longer want to think about the good times. It's as if they were merely a dream, and the nightmare is real.

"Gentlemen," Andre says, calling attention to us. "I'm sure you remember my sweet pets," he tells the guests. "Since the end of the Savage regime, I've slowly taken over and changed how things are run. Volkov may want things to be different in Russia, but I don't agree with his practices."

"You're going against the Bratva?" One man looks shocked at this, and I can't deny the mention of the Russian mafia doesn't instil me with calm.

"I am taking a stance," he says. "We have people watching us. The FBI are closing in on the Russians. I haven't told them because I want their business."

"What about those clowns who call themselves the Fallen?" another man asks before sipping on his red wine. There is refinement in this room. Elegance. But just like the house, there is a sinister core, which is slowly rotting away.

"They're nowhere near finding us. We've led them on a wild goose chase. I think we should set up the new auction to celebrate the holidays."

"Come." Andre tugs at our leashes and we follow behind. We know what's about to happen. The four of us lower to our knees. There may not be violence tonight, but there are other things that happen, which sends revulsion through me. We are here to entertain, to do their bidding, and we'll most likely be intimate with each other so they can appreciate the show. "It's time to enjoy ourselves. We will talk auctions later."

"Sir," one guard calls to Andre. "New delivery from Bragan," he says as he steps aside and they pull a girl into the room. She's got long blond hair that hangs in tangled waves down her back. Her pale skin is shimmering, and since the guards are also drenched, it seems it must have rained. I watch her shiver as she regards the room, dressed in only a pair of denim shorts and a white top that has now gone see-through. Her bra, a bright pink colour, is clearly visible.

"What do we have here?" Andre stops inches from her. He tips the gilr's head back as he assesses her. His touch causes her to shudder and shake. And yet, she doesn't speak. "What is your name, *chérie*?"

CHAPTER THREE

Tye

I pull up the photo I've kept of Einin. It's been sittin' on my computer desktop for as long as I can remember. And when it opens, I stare at her smilin' face.

The fair has brought the crowds to Ballycastle. Lammas has been a tradition in Ballycastle since before I was born, bein' held here for about four hundred years. The town comes alive, and the people who sell their goods are eager to make money. Even though the town itself has a fair few tourists throughout the year, this is one of the biggest days when we can show off what we're made of.

Most tourists who pass through come to visit the Giant's Causeway, but this is an event closer to the heart. Somethin' the people of the town can do to reap the benefits.

"Are we goin'ta get some sweets? Ma wants me to get the fresh bread, but then I'll have to run it home before we head to the beach," Einin says as she looks up at me. She's stood beside me, just like she always is.

We met when we were kids. Not exactly neighbours, but close enough that I would see her from my bedroom window when she was playin' in her ma's garden.

"Aye, we'll get sweets and bread," I tell her. "Then we'll take the loaves home to yer ma before comin' back out. I think the lads are goin'ta the beach now, anyway. We can join them later."

"I'm goin'ta get the soda bread fer Ma." Einin wades off through the crowds, her bright pink jumper standin' out, so I can thankfully find her once I'm done here.

I stop at the stall with the best sweets and cakes. But there, on the table amongst the delicious lookin' items, is what I'm lookin' for. Yellaman sits waitin' for me and I smile. The honeycomb toffee that's one of Einin's favourites is what I'm gettin' her. The stuff is far too sweet fer my likin'.

I buy two small bags and head off to find her. On my way, I stop at a stall that has rings, and for a long while, I stare at one of them. The wee stone shimmers with blue and green patterns.

"What are yer wantin' fer that one?" I ask as I stare at the pretty ring.

The older man glances to where I'm pointin' and smiles. "Fer ye, I'll make it fifty pound." It's all my savin's. "All right," he says as he watches my expression. "I'll do it for forty. How's that sound?"

"Grand." I can't stop smilin'. Einin will love it. She's into all these crystals and shite.

Once I've completed the transaction, I go to find her. But before she can spy the present, I hide the ring in my pocket. I'll give it to her tonight. And then I'll make a promise I have been wantin' to tell her fer a wee while now.

All I can hope is she's not goin'ta think I'm an eejit.

I shake my head free of the memory while I pull open my desk drawer. There, in the wee box, is the ring I bought. It's been there ever since I moved into the club. And it will stay there until I think she's ready.

Sighin', I get back to work. The emails I found glare at me from the screen. They're sellin' her on Christmas feckin' mornin'. These sick bastards are evil personified. They all deserve the feckin' wrath of Monster. And I'll gladly help.

I knew evil was out there. I find it daily while searchin' the dark web. But this is somethin' else.

Tradin' in human lives as if it's nothin' more than a transaction of livestock. They're talkin' about these women as if they're possessions.

I've always considered Einin mine. Since the moment I realised I loved her. But the idea of buyin' her, of goin' into an auction and biddin' on someone makes me sick.

Monster reaches my office just as we're about to leave. "Tye," he says my name with a grave tone. "When we get in there, I don't want ye puttin' yerself in danger. We work as a team, a family."

"Aye." I nod with conviction.

"If the shite hits the fan, and we need to leave, we feckin' walk out," he tells me. "Do ye understand me?" I've seen him give orders to the men before a ride out, but I've never been the focus of his command, not for a long while.

I look right into his eyes and nod. "Aye, I understand."

He squeezes my shoulder, a form of affection from the Pres who is always so serious. There are times I've seen him soften, but it's only when he's with Miren. The brothers see him when he's workin' mostly, which means his warmth is reserved for moments like these. "Grand. I don't need ye gettin' yerself killed."

"I'm not gettin' myself killed today, Monster." All I

can think of is holdin' her. Once I've freed Einin, she can focus on a future that was stolen from her.

"Right then. We don't need to lose ye." He stares at me, and a small grin forms on his mouth, as if he's happy with my answer, but stops. "And neither does she."

The thought of leavin' Einin doesn't sit well with me. My gut churns with anxiety. "I know. My focus is on gettin' her away from that bastard. I've done nothin' more than think about her for six feckin' years, and now is the time to do somethin' about her bein' hurt. I always thought of myself as her protector."

"And ye will be. It's the same way I feel about Miren. Ye're a good lad, Tye." He slaps me on the back in a show of camaraderie.

When I joined the club, Monster was the one person who vouched for me before everyone else. I met him in a bar in Belfast one night. He was drownin' his sorrows in a pint of Guinness while I was hittin' the Jameson. We talked about shite that didn't delve too deep—football and bikes. But I could tell he was hurtin' and I'm pretty sure he could see right through my façade.

That's when he asked me if I needed a place to stay. It was then I found my new family. He took me in and welcomed me along with the rest of the club. The brothers never questioned him. They took one look at me, and I became one of them.

Three months later, I patched in as Tech. And I'm still there. I can't see myself leavin' anytime soon. And that's what worries me. If Einin decides I'm what she wants but she doesn't feel at home at the club, I'm goin'ta have ta decide.

As if he can read my mind, Monster says, "Once we get her out of there, it's her choice whether she stays with us."

It's somethin' I'd been considerin' myself. What if she walks away from me again? But I know there's no doubt I'll allow her the choice. I'm not forcin' her to be anythin' she doesn't want to be. Even if I love her more than life itself.

"I've always loved her," I admit slowly. "But she'll always be free ta decide whether or not she stays with us. I understand that."

For six long years, I'd thought she'd moved on. Was convinced of it. I can't deny it broke me more than I thought. I was still young when I said goodbye to her.

"Then let's go get yer girl," he tells me with a smile before walkin' out of the office. I grab my things and follow right behind him. I never thought I'd live a day where I see Einin again. But now that we're about to head to France with the help of Venier, I'm anxious.

By the time we arrive in France, I'm worried. We took too long to get here. My mind is racin' with thoughts of what's about to happen. Our cut off to get to Einin is tomorrow, and I'm not sure what we'll find when we get to the house.

I've tracked the man who took her, right down to his feckin' blood type. And I'm goin' to make sure he pays. Monster wanted to get MI5 involved, but I wanted Einin safe before we called the peelers. They'd only want to question her, ask her shite that would surely only traumatise her. And that's not happenin' under my watch.

The bikes are loud as we rumble down the road. It was better for us to travel in a group, not knowin' what would happen once we arrived at the compound in the South of France. It's feckin' cold, but I can't deny it's beautiful out here.

All my life, I've never travelled. I stayed in Ireland because it was my home. I didn't think to leave. No other country called to me. And even though I can admit it's not too bad out here, I still have the ache in my gut to be on the Emerald Isle.

For a long time, I thought I should follow in Einin's footsteps. I wanted nothin' more than to see her again, but when I didn't hear from her after she'd left, I let her go. Regret sits heavily in my chest when I consider my mistakes. If I had reached out, if I had only just tried to find her, I would have saved her long ago.

There's not too much out here, so when you see us in biker cuts and hear the rumble of our bikes, we stand out. And it's pretty feckin' obvious we're not ye're average lad.

If anyone was wantin' complete privacy, this is the perfect place to be. It explains how this bastard has a compound of stolen women out here. There have been no raids on the house in question. Plus, when I investigated it, I found he's been payin' off law enforcement to turn a blind eye.

I snap my attention back to the present day when Monster slows down. As each of the men put on the breaks, Rebel and Racer are stopped in front of me. Monster swings his leg over his bike, and I realise he's comin' for me.

I'm anxious, he can understand that, but for him to just stop for no other reason than to check on me, it's frustratin' me. Only because we're within reachin' distance of the compound.

"Are ye ready fer this?" Monster asks when he stops in front of me.

Noddin', I say, "Aye. Never been more ready fer anythin' in my whole life." It's the truth. I want my girl now, and I want her safe.

"And ye remember what I told ye. Don't play the feckin' hero. Things will work out. We'll get her out of there. It's not long to go before we reach that compound and I'm not sure what we're goin'ta find."

"I don't want to think what's in there," I say. "The girls may not even know what's goin' on. From what I can tell, these arseholes are violent, they have no qualms about hurtin' those they *own*," I spit the word as if it's poison on my tongue.

"I'm goin'ta enjoy hurtin' them," Sully says from beside me, with a sinister grin curlin' his lips. "Nothin' like makin' a bastard pay for his sins."

"Now that sounds like fun," Rev adds, his voice filled with rage.

The man may be a chaplain, but that doesn't mean he doesn't like gettin' his hands dirty. I've been a witness to a few criminals who've been questioned by him. We've each had our time in the warehouse. Monster believes that no one person runs the club, even though he's the President. He's always made us feel as if we're equal, as if we all have a say in what goes on.

"Then let's ride." Monster heads back to his bike.

The rumble of the engines vibrate through me. My fingers grip the handlebars tight in a white-knuckle hold. I'm tense. My thoughts are with Einin. Monster is right. We don't know what we're ridin' into. But I would enter hell and face the devil himself if it means savin' her.

CHAPTER FOUR

Eirin

By the time we're taken back to our rooms, I've overheard more information about the upcoming auction which is taking place tomorrow—Christmas day. I didn't want to believe it, but they've confirmed there'll be new girls brought in. I'm still curious why the twins are here. Most of the homes I've been in over the years have only ever had young women.

The room is chilly tonight, and I slip under the covers, knowing that soon the bedroom door will be locked. We're kept like pets, but even if we were to get out of our rooms, there are so many guards around, there's no chance of escape. I've heard whispers about those who try. They don't make it out of the dungeon, which sits under the house.

Ice trickles down my spine when I consider this. I've experienced horrors before. When I think about all the times I was chained, beaten, and forced to do things with men, I realise nothing could scare me again. At least, that's what I think.

But these men are a different kind of human. If they're human at all. I wonder if the Devil walks amongst us and he's recruited them. An army of evil, walking the earth.

Curling into a ball, I bring my knees to my chest and close my eyes. When I wake tomorrow, I'm pretty sure any gifts I find will come at a price. Nothing in life is free, not in our lives.

For so long, I prayed for a miracle. Ma always told me God would be there when I needed him most, but it's all a lie. I've prayed to an entity that doesn't exist. At least, my belief has diminished over the years. And now, it's died. I no longer pray. I no longer ask for someone to save me, because I realise nobody is listening.

As much as I wished Tye would look for me, I'm

sure he's moved on by now. It's been so long, I doubt he even thinks of me. I couldn't keep in contact with him like I promised. He probably thinks I've moved on, that I've forgotten about him. But all these years, I replay that kiss in my mind. It's the only time I feel happy when I remember how his body felt against me. His lips tasted like sweets and his touch burned me like a fire raging through a forest.

I always teased him, telling him he was like the sun, scorching everything that got too close. And I got burned. I never admitted my feelings to him. I couldn't, because I wanted him to make the first move if he wanted to. When he kissed me, I thought he would ask me to stay, or he'd tell me he was coming with me. That he'd follow.

But he never did.

Maybe it was his da, perhaps it was his choice, but I lost the connection when I was taken. I think now about what-ifs that no longer help my mindset. They only seem to drag me deeper into the darkness, and I am losing the will to escape.

The last time I truly fought was last year. Before I finally allowed myself to forget about ever finding freedom. I was exhausted. I wanted nothing more than to die in the room the old captor kept me in.

I was bound in a bedroom with no window, he had stripped me bare. I would shiver in the cold, and when the men entered, the space became drenched in darkness and draped in violence.

"She's a pretty one," one man says. I'm not sure how many there are because I'm blindfolded, but I know for certain he *is here. My captor. The man who bought me is filled with evil. More than I want to consider. It's in his eyes. Like flames dancing in the darkness. When he glares at me, I see it. There's a devil inside him that's awake and hungry.*

"She's one of my best. I only got her a year ago," my captor says in his thick American accent. "She was too much for her old owner, but now that she's here, I've enjoyed making her cry and scream. But she hasn't lost her fire. Anything you want to do, you can. She fights beautifully as well."

"Mmm, it seems you've struck gold, Savage," another man utters beside me. He's so close to my left ear, I can taste the alcohol on his breath as it wafts over my face. "I think we should take her to your place."

"No," my captor, Savage, says. His name aptly fits him. The man is a brute. I've been kept in a cell, in a dungeon, since he purchased me. I didn't think I'd been flown all the way to America, but all of them have a similar accent. "My sons have their own toys to play with," he says to his guests. "This one," he murmurs as he touches my chin and I realise

he's right in front of me. "Is mine." His presence hovers over me like a dark, stormy cloud. The warmth of his body makes me recoil, which only causes the men to laugh out loud.

I can't go very far. My ankles are bound and so are my wrists. I'm nothing more than a toy for them to play with. The scars are both physical and emotional, and I doubt they'll ever heal.

"I think we need to get this party started," one of the men speaks. "Soon enough, they'll want to start the damn auction."

"We can, but she needs to be in good condition. No bruises and cuts," my captor warns, his voice dark, dangerous even.

I've overheard him mention an auction, which I know is when they'll sell me to a new owner. Every six months, we move, we're sent somewhere new if the price is right. If not, the girls that are left are killed in front of us before we are sent to our new owners.

I'm dragged from the nightmare by shouting and gunshots. I'm not sure what's going on, but I burrow further under the covers. The thought of violence erupting has me tense. Suddenly, my bedroom door flies open, and I'm practically dragged from the bed.

"Come," one of the men shouts.

He pulls me out into the hallway, and I'm stumbling after him as he grips my wrist. His fingers dig in harshly, causing me to whimper in pain. My gaze flicks around. I'm trying to locate Missy. Or the twins. But they aren't anywhere to be found.

"What's happening?" I mumble, trying to tug free from his hold, but the man is far stronger than I am. "Please?" Tears burn my eyes, but I fight them back. I don't need to show weakness. Fear already has a hold of me, and knowing my life is about to change once again makes me anxious.

"Move." He stops and shoves me into a room.

I don't see Missy or the twins, which makes my gut churn. If I'm being sold right now, or stolen once again, I'm not going to make it through. I can't. Just when I thought things were calming down. I have a new owner who doesn't hurt me, friends who went through the same thing as I have, and now I'm being thrown into turmoil again.

I glance over my shoulder to find the doors shut. There are still gunshots ringing through the air. We're all huddled in a corner. My hands are shaking as I shut my eyes so tight, I see white behind the lids.

There aren't any guards in the room, and I wonder briefly if we can make a break for it. The veranda doors are glass. All it would take is something to shatter them. I'm not foolish enough to think they'd leave the doors unlocked. It would be far too easy.

But getting out of the house is one task. Another is racing down the garden to the fence where we may be captured before we can even smell freedom. The noise outside the room is getting louder. Panic sets in. My heart thumps against my ribs. It's a reminder of where I am and what could possibly happen.

Nothing good.

Nothing good at all.

When silence finally falls, my stomach drops. There isn't a sound on the other side of the door, and I'm not sure if it's for the best. Me, along with the other ten girls, sit and wait.

It's as if we're waiting for the reaper to come through the door and take us to a better place. Anything would be better than being a captive to bad men. When the door swings open, we all jump.

"In here," the man at the threshold calls. He's not in uniform, so I don't know if he's a peeler or if he's like one of the devils I've come across in the years since I've been taken.

"What the fuck?" Another voice comes from the entrance hall.

The guard who brought me into this room was clever. He dragged me through the back of the house, while avoiding main entrance hall.

"Agent," one of the men in uniform finally appears and my chest tightens. *Agent?* That means the peelers are here. They've found us. "We can't find Andre," the uniformed man says. "There's no sign of him down in the basement or up in any of the rooms."

"And the girl and the twins?" the agent asks, glancing over his shoulder.

He must be talking about Missy, James, and Josh. They're the only ones I can think of. They're my friends, and if Andre took them, it means they hold higher value than we do. He may have something even more dangerous up his sleeve for them.

Fear sets in when more men storm into the room. The agent offers us a look filled with sadness and pity. "It's all going to be okay," he says as he stops in front of us. "We need to talk to each of you, but for now, I'd like you to go with my men."

"Where are the twins and Missy?" I ask, fear holding me tightly in its icy grip. There were times over the past few months where I didn't think I would make it. I was convinced it would be the end of me, but those three stood by me, supported me.

"We're not sure," he tells me. I don't know where the agent's from, but I can pick out his accent is clearly

American. “We have a team on that,” he continues. “Don’t worry, we’ll find them.”

His assurance doesn’t calm my heart rate, and it thuds against my ribs, travelling slowly up into my throat and tries to suffocate me. Panic sets in and my breathing comes in short bursts.

The agent offers me his hand, and when I lift my gaze, I find kindness instead of anger and seething. Over the years, men have looked at me as if I was nothing more than a piece of shite under their shoe.

That is, until they wanted something. Until they needed something. Seven long years, and I’m free. I haven’t left this house yet, but I know I’m free just from looking into the man’s eyes. I take his hand and he helps me to stand. Then, I follow him from the room to find commotion in the entrance hall. There are bodies slain on the floor, a reminder of what took place just outside the room we were locked in.

I glance up, trying not to look at the men lying there. Guards who enjoyed pushing us around, now no longer breathing. It’s only when the agent stops and speaks to someone and they reply does my heart stutter.

“Any sign of our girl?” The familiar accent comes towards me, filters over to my ears, and it settles there like the warmth of a fire on a cold winter’s day. A reminder of home.

"I'm sorry," the agent says. "There are a handful of girls and two boys missing. We have a feeling the asshole took them with him when he fled. Someone tipped him off, which means we have a mole. We will have an inquiry once we're back in the States."

"We'll find her," the other man says, his thick Belfast brogue rumbling through his chest. And then, the agent steps aside and I look up into dark eyes. "What's yer name?" he asks me.

"Einin," I tell him, and he smiles before he steps aside.

There, standing just behind the enormous man with broad shoulders, is a face I never thought I'd see again. It's the face of the boy I fell in love with, only he's older and has stubble on his jawline. But those eyes, the familiar gaze that used to make my teenage heart thrum like hummingbird wings.

It's Tyrion.

CHAPTER FIVE

Tye

I can't find my words.

They're stuck in my throat somewhere, so I don't say anything.

When we got the call from the States that the FBI were on a case that was leading them to France, we couldn't believe our luck. They've been tracking a shipment of girls who arrived here a few days ago, and we followed along. Having connections in high places allows you certain privileges. Also, it helps I was able to do some hacking for them that closed a case a year ago.

Agent Ramirez wanted to storm the house first. I didn't want to wait, but Monster put the command out and I had to obey. I waited outside, my nerves shot to hell, but here I am, finally in front of her.

I didn't expect her to look the same, but she's even more beautiful than I remember. She is still the same girl I fell in love with. The same girl who's held onto my feckin' heart all this time.

I've changed. No longer the scrawny lad she met at school. Before Einin left, I'd been workin' out, focusin' on weights and tryin'ta build muscle, but I didn't have the bulk I do now. I haven't shaved in a couple of days, and I know I have a few battle scars.

She stares at me for so long, I'm not sure she even recognises me.

It's as if time has come to a standstill and I'm havin' an out of body experience. With the commotion around us, I don't even flinch. I don't see my brothers movin' around the enormous room. All I see is her.

The peelers are shoutin' orders while Monster and the rest of the Royal Bastards work to get the girls out of the house. They know this is monumental for me. I almost lost my shit when I knew I had to wait to see her, to find her. I wasn't sure what we would come across when we walked in here, but she doesn't look hurt. I'm prayin' she isn't. I'm prayin' for so much in the moments that pass, I'm not sure God is even listenin'.

"What are you doing here?" Are her first words to me.

For a moment, I think she's angry, but then I see the tears in her eyes. They make those familiar orbs shimmer. Hazel brown with flecks of olive green.

"I found ye," I finally mutter while takin' a few steps towards her. She doesn't flinch. She doesn't even blink. Her gaze focused on me. I stop inches from her.

"I stopped prayin' a long time ago, big man," she whispers before I pull her into my arms and she falls into my chest. She twines her hands behind my back, and she holds on as if I'm about to disappear. The nickname she gave me all those years ago settles in my chest. It's like comin' home. Like walkin' into ye house after a long day at work, and the warmth holds ye in its familiar grip.

"I didn't know ye were missin', wee bird," I tell her, usin' her nickname I'd given her on her sixteenth birthday. "When I left Ballycastle at nineteen, I never looked back."

It's the truth. Da told me that I only come back if it's to bury him. I fought him, I argued for months, but he didn't want to hear anythin' 'bout it. So, I finally appeased the old man and walked out. I knew he only said what he did because he didn't want to see me stuck in the small town. I knew he'd always felt trapped there, having taken over the shop from his da, and he wanted a better opportunity for me.

It was the first time in my life I did listen to him. Even though I check in with him every day, I haven't gone back.

"Tye," Monster calls to me, breaking the spell that's so clearly captured both Einin and myself. "Let's get her home."

"Aye," I say with a nod and turn back to her. "We'll go home. To Belfast."

"Ye're part of a motorcycle gang now?" Einin asks with a small smile, lifting her brow.

I take her hand and tangle my fingers with hers.

"They're family," I tell her. "Let's get yer things and head out. I'm knackered."

We walk up the stairs, and she heads to a bedroom that looks fancy enough. I wonder if they put the girls in rooms like this to make them feel comfortable, so they don't fight when the violence comes. But then again, I'm not sure what has happened to any of the women we saved today.

I want to ask her, but now isn't the time. Once we're home, safely, I'll sit her down. She needs to talk about what happened. I have to know what she's been through. I've been in contact with a group who call themselves The Fallen. They'd been searchin' for their sister and twin brothers, who were stolen when they were much younger than Einin was. When I mentioned the agent was comin' out here, I put them in contact with him.

Hopefully, they have a happy endin' just like I have. Einin turns once she's packed her shite and smiles. "I'm ready to go." Even though her lips are tilted up at the corners, there's sadness in her eyes.

"I know ye're not all right, and things have been shite, but you're safe now. I'm never lettin' you outta my sight," I tell her. It's the truth. I can't lose her again. Ever. "That day on the beach, when I kissed ye," I whisper when she nears me, "I meant it. I meant every feckin' moment."

She stops in front of me. Instinctively, I take her rucksack and swing it over my shoulder, but I don't break eye contact.

"I know," is all she says before she takes my hand and we head back down to where the rest of the men are waitin'.

The brothers only offer a greetin' when I introduce each of them in turn. I know they're curious to learn about the new girl in our world. I wasn't lyin' to her when I said they're family. We run on loyalty and strength.

"Rebel, Sully, Racer." I point at the three brothers in the front. "This is Einin," I say as I glance down at her. Each of them offers a tip of their head before I continue namin' the brothers who are stood further back. Once the introductions are done, I head to my bike and help Einin on behind me.

Monster returns from talkin' to the agent who follows behind him. "Are ye all ready to go?"

"Aye," Sully responds first, but Rebel steps forward. I hadn't thought about how he would be doin'. I didn't see Callia, and they didn't mention her name.

"Boss!" a voice shouts from the house and they turn to him.

From behind the peeler who's standing on the threshold of the mansion, a girl steps out, and for a moment, I think it's Callia.

Her gaze lands on Rebel's and I realise it is her. Only her hair isn't blond, it's a pastel pink and longer, much longer. She races into Rebel's arms and sobs. The sound of her anguished cries has me pulling Einin into my arms. I'm thankful she seems almost normal, as if she's okay. For the most part, I think she is. The man who took Callia from us was the devil himself. Which makes me wonder about the man who owns this house, who owns Einin right now.

"Let's go," Monster announces and we get on our bikes.

The rumble of all the engines at once vibrates through me. With Einin's arms around me, I pull away, following behind in formation with the rest of the brothers.

Our connection with the Italians has allowed us use of their private plane. Venier is a good lad. Since he's taken over from his father, for the most part, things seem to be runnin' smoothly. So, when we get to the hangar, the aircraft is waitin' to take us back to Ireland. The FBI can question Einin when they meet us in Belfast. I don't want her to be here longer than she needs to. They have so many captives to question before they need Einin.

The girls have been through hell. The moment we get home, though, they're going to need to sit down and take us through everythin'. I'm not stupid enough to think Patrick will just walk away from his daughter. There has to be a reason he's let Callia go. Somethin' doesn't feel right when we board, and once we're settled, it's Rebel who is first to question it.

"Why did Patrick let ye come home?" His voice is chilled as he regards Callia.

The doubt in his eyes is enough to have me needin' my laptop. I have to do some diggin'. The itch of not bein' able to find information quickly is frustratin'.

"He said he... He told me he would be back in Belfast soon. And when he does return, he's going to take the whole club out. He left me here to pass on the message." Callia glances at Monster, and somethin' flickers in her gaze. Her expression is pained. There must be more to it, and I have a feelin' it has to do with him. She looks at Rebel, who's at her side. "I want to go home."

But Monster steps forward. "Why did ye go to yer father in the first place? What is he holdin' over yer head?" Monster asks, leanin' his forearms on the small table between them.

The air is thick with worry, the tension is feckin' stiflin'. It's times like these that make me feel more at ease with a whirrin' computer than human interaction. But I haven't let go of Einin's hand since we got off my bike. I doubt I could ever let her go.

"I had to go. My choice has nothing to do with you. It's done now," Callia says with conviction clear in her tone. But she doesn't say anythin' more about her choice. "What I can tell you is that there were meetings being scheduled. They're meant to take place over the next couple of months. He's aimin' for the new year, March. He said he needed time to set everything up. He had a call from someone in Italy because I overheard him speaking in Italian, but when I tried to listen in, he caught me and..." Callia turns to the window, her shoulders slumpin', and my gut twists.

"What is it, Callia? Ye know ye can tell us anythin'," Monster implores, while Rebel rages beside her. His hands are in white-knuckled fists as he glares.

Rebel's not angry at her. I know he's furious because of what she's been through. The bastard hasn't told her he loves her, but everyone else in the club can see it. I'm not sure why, but he's been far too slow to react, to admit his feelings.

"He did his own form of punishment," she whispers.

A shudder races through her; I can see her whole body shakin'. I've come close to killin' once before, and today, a second wave of that same emotion rolls through me. I want to hurt the bastards who did this. I want to make them bleed.

My early life was spent in a small town where everyone knew everyone else. There weren't any secrets, but people were happy. There was a sense of support, of community. We didn't have brawls or any of that shite that happens in the city. But right now, violence runs through my veins. I got my girl, but I'm willin' to fight for my family.

Since I joined the club, I've learnt that blood doesn't always mean loyalty. I've watched fellow brothers struggle with their own lives, their own pasts. It's not been easy. I've come to love each of them. And I realised, not long after patching in, I would do anything for these men. And the women who are part of the club.

I've watched Monster dole out his fair share of punishments over the years, and I've never understood it, not fully.

But in the past, I had nothing to fight for.

Now, I do.

CHAPTER SIX

Einin

Ireland feels different to any other place I've been. Not that I've travelled much. But the city of Belfast has a character. As if it's alive, with a beating heart and a soul. On the back of Tye's motorbike, the city flies by as we weave through the traffic.

The fresh air smells different, and I don't know if it's because I'm free or because I'm with Tye. When we were young, he was always a foundation for me. He gave me advice when I needed it, and he was there when I needed someone to talk to. Our friendship grew from the first day we met, until the moment I got on the bus for the airport. My flight was meant to take me to London. I didn't think I'd ever see him again. I was convinced I would die in one of the houses I was sent to. Seven long years have passed, and holding onto him as he speeds down the streets feels like I've finally come home.

We pull up to a large property. The walls are high, with security cameras pointing at us. There are two young lads at the gates who offer a nod to Tye. They allow him entry, and we ride up a long drive that takes us to a house so big, it reminds me of those I was taken to over the past few years.

All the men who owned us were rich, and they made sure we knew how far beneath them we were. As captives, we had nothing but the clothes on our backs. It was only my most recent captor who bought me clothes. He wanted to ensure we portrayed a certain image to his friends.

I don't expect the welcome as we step inside the entrance. There are Christmas decorations that sparkle as Tye leads me through to a lounge. There are other women all settled on the couches, and one of them leaps to her feet when Callia walks in. They hug, and I can tell they're good friends.

"That's Miren," Tye whispers in my ear. "She's Monster's ol' lady." The woman is almost pixie-like in her beauty. Breathtaking.

"She's really beautiful." I don't realise I say it out loud, but Tye squeezes my hand, causing me to look up at him.

"You're beautiful," he says with a smile before leading me to the woman. "Miren, this is Einin." He releases my hand, allowing me to greet Miren.

"It's so good to have you here. I'm so happy they found you," she tells me and then suddenly pulls me into a hug.

The warmth of her should calm my erratic pulse, but I'm not used to people touching me. Not even Missy could hug me most times. It takes a lot for me not to flinch at someone's hands or fingers on me. It's only Tye who doesn't bring about that need to run, to hide.

"It's been a long while since I was home," I tell her. The tears of relief I've been holding onto burn my eyes, and I have to fight to keep them at bay. I don't want to cry in front of someone I don't know.

"Well, you're here now, and you'll be safe," she tells me with a smile. "Tye will show you to a room. You can get some rest."

I know it's Christmas tomorrow. It will be a day of

happiness for me because I'm no longer a prisoner. I'm free.

Tye takes my hand and smiles. "I'll introduce ye to everyone tomorrow. We're going to have lunch with everyone. All the ol' ladies cook, and then we settle around the table."

As he speaks, I can't help but take in the home. My new home. It's an enormous place with little hallways off in every direction. We take the staircase up to the first floor; it has long corridors with doors down either side leading off into the distance. I haven't seen a house like this in Ireland, besides the castles that sit on acres of land.

This comes fairly close to one of those.

"So, is Monster the President?" I ask, recalling the patch I saw on his cut.

"Aye, he's in charge," Tye says. "Then there's Rebel, who's VP. He's second-in-command. We each have our roles here, but we're all a family. Part of a team, rather than being beneath anyone."

"And what are you?"

"I do tech," he tells me. "Anything ye want online, I can find it. Some things are easy to find." This time, he stops and looks at me. "And other things are harder."

He steps aside and opens a door that leads into

a bedroom. It's cosy, with a large double bed and a window that overlooks the garden. The sun is low on the horizon. We have been travelling for hours, and as the early evening takes a hold of the day, the sky has turned darker.

"But you found me," I whisper, responding to Tye's explanation of his job.

I turn from the window to find him watching me. His arms folded across his chest. Arms that are much bigger than those of the boy I remember. I notice ink peeking out from under his T-shirt, and I wonder what it is, and if he has more.

"I did." His voice is lower, a gentle rumble. I haven't thought about what would happen if I ever saw him again. To be honest, I'd given up thinking about a life of freedom. "I'll leave ye to rest. There's a bathroom across the way," he says with a gesture towards the door behind him. Towels are in the cupboard, and if ye need anythin', give me a shout."

With a small smile, he shuts the door. I'm alone. Instead of wanting to sleep, I'm curious about my new space. A bedroom that's warm and so very different to the ones I'm used to.

I go to the tables on either side of the bed and open both sets of drawers. They're empty. There's a wardrobe with a few pairs of jeans hanging on one side, and on the other are wooden shelves. A couple of hoodies are folded and placed on the middle shelf, and I grab one and throw it on.

Deciding quickly, I unpack my meagre belongings and smile when I step back to take in the small, yet personal touch. I search a dressing table but can't find any towels, so I head to the bathroom Tye mentioned.

I notice this part of the house is quieter than the lounge. Once in the bathroom, I lock the door behind me. I find the towels and grab one before stripping off and turning on the taps. The shower warms quickly. Under the spray, I close my eyes and allow the water to wash away the past. There were so many horrific things I've witnessed over the three years. I'm thankful, for the most part, I wasn't hurt like other girls were. Yes, I was whipped when I didn't comply on occasion, but I got off luckier than most.

I wash my hair before lathering my hands in shower gel. I rub every part of me until I'm happy I'm clean, and then I stand under the warm spray for a long while. With my eyes shut, my memories take a hold of me.

When I was first taken, I woke up in America. my captor made sure I knew I would never get home if I tried to run. There were nights I would wake up with someone watching me, someone in my room because they'd paid to be there. A man, sometimes a couple. There was never any intimacy, and I always wondered what their strange kinks were.

It was a strange, scary time, when I never knew if they would hurt me or not. They would want me to wear certain items of clothing that would cause me to shudder. And that's when they'd touch, gently at first, and then rougher.

It was only when I was sold to a man who called himself the Judge that things turned more violent, darker. It was a short time. I was there only a few months before Andre bought me at an auction. Which brings me here. Home.

I shut off the taps and dry off. My need to be in my room takes a hold of me. My breathing comes in short spurts, and I realise I'm going to have a panic attack. They started not long after I was taken. It was what always got me into trouble. I couldn't help it. They came at the most inopportune times. As much as I wanted to fight them, to breathe through them, I couldn't because they would take over.

I wrap myself in the towel before grabbing my clothes and rushing from the bathroom, only to slam into a hard, muscled frame. Tilting my head back, I lift my gaze and find Tye's gentle stare. His hands are on my arms, holding me steady as he smiles down at me.

"Where are ye rushin' off to?" he asks with a chuckle before he realises I'm in distress. "Come," he says quickly and leads me into the bedroom before shutting the door. "What's wrong? Einin, calm down. Breathe. Look at me, look into my eyes." His orders come quickly, and I obey so easily. It's there I find affection, in those familiar brown eyes.

When I'm finally able to breathe easier, Tye releases his hold on me. I step back slowly before placing a hand on his chest. The thrum of his heartbeat thuds against my palm. He was worried.

"I get those sometimes," I tell him.

His gaze trails over me then, and it's in that moment we both realise I'm naked. Only wrapped in a towel, I feel my cheeks warm as his gaze flickers with desire. I've never seen him look at me like that before. When we were younger, I had the biggest crush on Tye. But I was convinced he didn't feel the same, until the day he finally kissed me.

The memory of his lips on mine washes away all the dark thoughts I just had. And I'm left with my belly coiling with need. The feel of his body against mine races through my mind, and it's as if it happened yesterday.

"I better get dressed," I finally whisper, but Tye doesn't move.

His gaze finds my face again. "I know this probably isn't the right time to do this, but I've never been one to find the right moments for anythin'." He takes a step towards me, stopping inches from where I am. "I'm never goin' to let ye go, ever again," Tye whispers as his hand reaches for my face. He cups my cheek gently while running his thumb over my lips. "You've always been mine, Einin," he tells me with the confidence I fell in love with all those years ago.

I can't deny it's true. I was always his. My young heart knew it before I had time to admit it. Whenever I looked at Tye, I knew I would be okay. He was there for me, he was more than just a friend. He was my first love. And I know even if I didn't get back here, even if he didn't find me, he would be my last love because he took my heart so many years ago.

As if he's reading my mind, Tye says, "Ye stole my feckin' heart, Einin. Fer six long years, I was so angry with ye. I thought ye'd taken it and run off, that ye didn't give a shite," he continues softly. "But it was my mistake. I shoulda fought fer ye."

"You couldn't have known," I whisper, my stare

locked on his. His touch is tender when he once again swipes along my lips.

"I shoulda known," he affirms as his brows furrow. His expression is pained, as if it hurts him to think he didn't realise I was taken. "Never again." The two words are a vow, a promise, and I know he means it because the one thing Tyrion O'Connell is known for is that he never breaks a promise.

For a moment, I ache for him to kiss me. To swipe all those memories of darkness away, but he steps back and drops his hand. I shiver when he's no longer close, his warmth stolen from me.

"Ye should be restin'," he says. "I've just brought ye up somethin' to eat. I'll come fer ye in the mornin'." With a smile, he turns and leaves.

The door is shut, I'm alone, and yet, I don't want to be. Deep down, I want to run after him and ask him to stay, but I know he won't, because he would want me to heal. The thing is, he's the one who can fix me. I'm sure of it.

So, for now, I make myself at home because I'm not leaving him again.

Ever.

CHAPTER SEVEN

Tye

Last night was difficult.

I didn't want to walk away from her, but I knew I had to. She needs time. There are things she's been through, things I don't know yet, which will still haunt her.

There's no doubt, though, I meant what I said. I'm not letting her go again. She's mine, always has been. Nobody is going to go near her, hurt her, ever again. Now I have her, she's here to stay.

"Merry Christmas, Tye," Miren says as she enters my

office with a mug of coffee.

"Thanks, love. Merry Christmas, to ye." It's early in the morning, not even six yet, but I'm working. She and Monster are happy. Watchin' them in love is like watchin' those feckin' romance movies. Her London accent is still strong when she speaks, but every now and then, she'll mimic Monster in some way, which makes me laugh.

Miren smiles as she looks over at me then says, "She's lovely."

"Aye." I nod. "She's always been like that. Just a bit shy, but there's a light inside her I fell in love with." I've never told anyone this before. Never admitted I loved her to anyone else but myself. Takin' the mug from Miren, I say, "Thanks."

"It's a special day today." Miren settles in one of the chairs beside me. "You should tell her how you feel. Not only to make yourself feel better, but just so she knows where you stand. If you never tell her, she'll always doubt it."

"Like Rebel?" I throw out, thinking about how he and Callia keep their feelin's bottled up and neither of them is happy. Callia still has secrets, I get that, but Rebel is the only one who would be able to break down her walls.

"Yes," Miren says. "Rebel's stubborn, but trust me, he'll come around at some point. There'll be a break in those walls. At times, it takes one scary moment, when you think you're going to lose the person you love to shatter every defence you've built around you."

"Thank you." She's right. I need to say the words, but I need to say them to Einin.

Miren leaves me with those thoughts to ponder as I scroll through information on Patrick. I've sent what I found through to Dante Savage. One of the men who works on the dark web. We came across each other one day while hackin' into surveillance and kept in touch.

Dante mentioned there was another hacker investigating the traffickin' ring. Known as the Fallen, they're three lads lookin' for missin' family members. I'm pretty sure, from the description they've sent through, it's the youngens that Ramirez was talkin' about. I hope they find them.

I work until eight before I head up with a cup of coffee to get Einin. She is probably enjoyin' a lie in, but we need to have a little heart-to-heart before we sit down with the family for Christmas lunch later.

When I reach her bedroom, I knock on the door, waitin' for her to reply. The moment it swings open and Einin is standin' on the other side, in a pair of pajamas and her messy hair, I can't help but smile.

"Mornin'," I greet her before offerin' her the hot drink. "Merry Christmas," I say, realisin' I didn't even wish Miren any season's greetin's. My thoughts were so wrapped up in Einin.

"Morning," she says with a smile, steppin' aside and allowin' me entrance. "Merry Christmas," Einin whispers with a happy smile. "I was about to get dressed and come down to see if I can help."

"No need." I turn to her and notice she's shut the door. I didn't expect her to be comfortable to be alone with me like this, but I'm thankful she is. "The other ladies have it covered."

She blows on the coffee before takin' a long sip. Her lashes flutter against her cheeks, and she makes a sound of pure satisfaction. A sound that makes my blood run hot and my cock throb. I want her to make all those sounds when I finally claim her. I would be a liar if I said I hadn't thought about it.

"We needed to talk," I finally say.

I'm anxious. My gut is churnin' as I consider what I'm about to say. There are so many things that are racin' through my mind, but I go to her and focus on those pretty feckin' eyes. They have always been my home. I would look at her and I'd know things would be all right.

Her dark brows furrow before she asks, "Is something wrong?"

"No, no, darlin'," I say quickly. "If I don't tell ye this now, I don't know when I'll get the courage again. I'm not a man who talks about emotions and all that shite." I run my fingers through my short hair and sigh. "I spent the past seven years convinced ye'd left me. I figured ye moved on with some college boy."

"Why would you think that?"

"I don't know." I turn away from her, ashamed of my stupidity. But she never told me she felt anythin'. Aye, our kiss was feckin' steamin' hot, but it coulda just been in the moment.

"I was taken to America for a short time," Einin finally admits. "I thought I was going to die there. They would do things to us. Make us wear certain clothes," she admits slowly. I turn to find her sittin' on the foot end of the bed. Her head lowered, her eyes on the floor. "We would either be clothed in outfits or naked. Bound. They would inspect us like we were livestock."

"Jesus," I hiss, anger takin' hold of me. My blood boilin' now for a different reason altogether.

"All those times, I would shut my eyes and think about being back in Ballycastle. I would go home, and you know what always got me through?" Now she looks up at me. Her eyes on mine.

"What?"

"You."

I didn't expect one word to change my thoughts. I never once imagined what it would be like to see her again, because when the first year passed without a word from her, I convinced myself she had moved on. She took my heart with her when she got on that bus, and I let her. I didn't fight it.

"Ye left, and I thought ye were done with me."

"When I told you Da wanted me to leave," she whispers, and the tears that form on her lashes cause her eyes to shimmer, "I lied."

"What do you mean?" My chest tightens with fear, worry that she could ever have lied to me. We always told each other the truth, no matter what. It was something we promised each other when our friendship started.

"Ma wanted me to leave because of ye," she admits. "I think deep down she knew I was falling for ye, and she didn't want me stuck in a small town for the rest of my life."

"She thought I'd end up like my da." The realisation hits me deep. She lied to stop me from getting hurt.

"Aye, but when she told Da about our friendship, he wanted to get involved. He was going to send men up to town to take care of the *problem*," Einin spits the last word with venom in her tone.

But my confusion must be clear on my face when she sighs and nods. But I ask anyway, "Men? What are ye talkin' about?"

But then she admits somethin' I wasn't expectin' from her. "My da was workin' with the Irish mob."

Pieces slot into place. It doesn't take long for me to place each one where they now belong. Einin's da was workin' for Bragan. Which means he believed his daughter would be kept safe, or so he thought.

"Did ye da ever get in contact with ye?"

"No. I mean, he was expecting me to arrive in London, but obviously I never got there." She takes another sip of her coffee while my brain works overtime. "Why? What are you thinking?"

"Feck," I curse out loud. "Bastard." I look at Einin, who's starin' at me, confused. "Come with me," I say before racin' from her bedroom and leavin' the door open behind me.

I make a beeline for my office, ignorin' Racer when I rush by him. He follows me to the office, and not long after, Einin enters as well.

I'm at my computer with the screen, trailin' through names. I type in Einin's da's name into my software and wait for it to pull up what I already know. It didn't take long for me to figure it out when she mentioned what happened.

"What's goin' on?" Racer asks when he flops into a chair and pulls out a smoke. The flick of his lighter has me turnin' my head. "What?"

"There's more to the feckin' story than I thought. I'm pretty sure Patrick was dealin' in women and girls for far longer than we anticipated." Sinéad and Patrick Bragan were runnin' the mob for years, until she took her baby and fled. Miren was the child who grew up not knowin' who her da was. At the same time, Einin's da didn't know his boss, Patrick, was a feckin' arsehole.

Patrick had Einin taken. It's the only explanation I can come up with. Her da must have confided in his boss thinkin' nothin' of it. But what worries me is that there was never any search goin' for her. If her da knew she was missin', why didn't he look for her? Why didn't he alert the peelers?

When I find what I'm lookin' for, the big picture is finally revealed. "Feckin' hell."

"What the feck are ye on about?" Racer asks again.

Spinnin' my chair to look at him, I explain, "When

Einin left for school, her da was the one who arranged the trip. But what I didn't know is Patrick was his boss. He was the one who said he'd get her to London. The emails between Patrick and George show somethin' else." I look at Einin. "Yer da was worried. He'd asked for Patrick's help to find ye, but by then, ye were on a plane out of the country. Patrick had promised five girls to the bastard across the pond."

"But wouldn't Da have known this? He worked for Patrick."

Shaking my head, I say, "No. Ye da believed the man he was workin' for was tryin'ta help him. He believed Patrick was searchin' for ye, but instead, he was rakin' in millions because ye were sold off before ye even said goodbye to ye ma."

"So, ye're tellin' me Patrick was sellin' the kids of his workers?" Racer leans forward, the cigarette hangin' from his lips as he speaks.

"Aye."

"And they asked him for help thinkin' he had the connections to find them, not the peelers." Racer deduces what I found and confirmed only moments ago.

It makes sense. If ye're workin' for a powerful man like Bragan, ye'd think he'd be the one to find yer loved one. The peelers don't do shite to help, so it's better to trust someone with criminal connections because he'd do anythin' to support us.

Einin flops into a chair. Her face is a picture of shock. I can't imagine what she must be feelin'. The thought of what she's been through is still fresh in my mind. I remember she said they did terrible things to the girls, which only makes me sick to my stomach.

I've never thought about violence as an answer, but the more I hear about what the world is really like, the more it's becomin' clearer to me that sometimes it's the only option. I may only be the tech in the club, but I have fists as well. And I ain't scared to get them bloody if I have to. And for Einin, I'll kill.

"I can't believe it."

"We need to have a meetin'." Racer is right. He pushes to his feet and looks at me. "I'll tell Monster what ye just said. He'll probably want to call church tonight."

"Aye, that's fine."

Racer leaves me and Einin in my office. So much for a chilled Christmas Day. All I wanted to do was relax with my girl, but I know that if we meet, we can get a plan together. I'm trackin' Bragan's contacts, and soon enough we'll find him. I know Callia said he was comin' for us, but if we can get to him first, we'll have the element of surprise.

Pushin' to my feet, I go to Einin and offer her my hands. She takes them with a smile. I pull her to her feet, and then, into my arms. Her gentle touch scorches me. She wraps herself around me, holdin' on as if she were sinkin' and I were her saviour. I will be. I am. And nothin' will ever stop me from bein' there for her.

Never again.

CHAPTER EIGHT

Einin

I've made a decision. I need him. I want him to make me forget. But now is not the time. Once we've spent time with his family, we can have our privacy. I want to tell him so many things. But they'll have to wait for now.

"I came to your room to tell you somethin' and I ended up workin'," Tye says as he steps back to look at me. "I can't lose ye," he confesses with a smile. "I've always felt as though ye were home. And ye need to know before we go out there and have the rest of them all fawnin' over you. I lo—"

"Wait," I stop him before he can say it. Even though I want to hear it, we should wait. I can't help but giggle at his confusion. "I doubt there'll be fawning. But we can talk about our feelings a bit later," I admit. "There has never been a day in my life since we met that I haven't wanted more from you, but patience will make it even better, once we get there."

There's shock written all over Tye's face, which makes me smile. I had never made it obvious to him how I felt. Mainly because I always thought I wasn't pretty enough or popular enough.

He was the bad boy who was just out of reach. So, I kept him close as his friend, hoping that one day I'd be able to see him happy. Even if it meant it wasn't with me.

"Why didn't ye ever tell me?"

Shrugging, I say, "It doesn't matter. Our friendship meant more to me than anything else. And if I had you like that, I didn't want to lose you over a stupid thing like feelings."

"Ach, that's hardly stupid is it?" His expression tells me everything I need to know. He isn't happy I didn't tell him.

"Aye, but you didn't tell me either," I throw back,

swatting him on the chest. "Anyways, it's done now. I know, and *you* know."

I hug him once more before leaning back to look into those cocoa eyes. Then, I rise up on my tiptoes to quickly press a kiss to his lips, which is too fast and we bash our teeth together. The awkward moment causes us both to laugh. It's the first time in years I can laugh with true happiness filling my heart.

"Let's get out there," Tye says, and I'm about to move when he captures my face in his hands and leans in. His lips find mine. It's a soft, gentle kiss. While his tongue sweeps along mine, every nerve ending in my body sparks to life. A reminder of our first kiss we shared on the beach comes to mind, and I smile against his mouth.

We finally make our way to the lounge where we find most of the guys and a few of the women and children. Miren is sitting beside Monster, while Callia is on a beanbag, watching Rebel and Racer.

"I'm Sully." A tall, tattooed man steps up to us. "It's nice to meet ye," he tells me. His dark hair is a mess of waves that hang to the nape of his neck, and his green speckled eyes shimmer.

"It's nice to meet you as well," I say while shaking his hand.

Every part of him that's exposed is inked, which brings my thoughts back to Tye and his tattoo.

"Brute, but you can call me Hades," another of the men says when he stops to greet me. "And that's Hadrian, or Rev." He points to a man who looks just like him. Twins. Hades and Rev are inked as well, from their necks down to their hands.

We settle in for a while. Everyone is chatting, drinking, and having a good time. Miren makes me feel welcome, and I find I'm feeling more comfortable than I was yesterday, or even earlier.

Eventually, the men head into an adjoining room to meet, or as they like to call it, church, while I get to know Miren and Callia. The rest of the women move around the house, some in the kitchen, others outside.

I help Miren set the table, while Callia ensures all the kids are seated at the smaller table as we get ready for lunch. I'm starving. I realise the last time I ate was last night when Tye brought me soup and a wee toastie.

Once the doors of the church open, the men file out and make their way straight to the table. Everyone is in high spirits. There's music filtering through the speakers as we all take our seats. I'm between Rev and Tye, feeling rather tiny since all these men are tall, broad-shouldered, and dangerous-looking.

I'm thankful I'm here. As I watch them all chatter, I can't help but feel a sense of ease. These were all strangers who have now come together to form a family. I grew up with Ma. It was always the two of us. There was no extended family, because when Ma fell pregnant at sixteen, her folks told her to leave. She met Da on the bus out of the small town she grew up in. He talked her into going further north, and she did. They fell in love quickly. Ma told me she lost the baby, but Da married her and told her one day they'd have a family. He still loved her then.

When I came along, it was a surprise, but something inside my da changed. Ma told me he would be out all night drinking while she was away all day working. And then, he left. They kept in touch through letters, but there was no longer love between them.

I glance at Tye, thankful he took so long to tell me he wants me. In my mind, I had convinced myself if we admitted our feelings too soon, I could've ended up alone like Ma.

"Ye all right?" Tye asks as we tuck into our food.

"Yes." I smile.

Hearing him say those three words will be a dream come true. I can't deny my teenage heart would have leapt from my chest if he'd said it back then. But it was worth the wait. It made being home, being here, so much better.

All the food is delicious. There's quite a spread. But having these men here to devour everything, I can see why the women have made so much. The banter is good fun, and everyone seems to be enjoying themselves.

"What'd ye get fer Miren?" Sully asks Monster.

"A baby," Racer throws out with a chuckle and receives a glare from his President. "What? It's true."

"Aye," Rebel chirps. "Bang on. It's because they can't stay out of the feckin' bedroom."

"Ye're a real charmer. Aren't ye, Racer?" Monster asks, his voice a deep rumble. But the rest of the men laugh out loud. There's love here. They may be teasing each other, but it's done with good intentions.

"I'm only feckin' wit ye." Racer holds up his hands in surrender.

"Eejit," Monster grumbles, while Miren leans in to whisper something in his ear that makes him smile.

The rest of the lunch is just as rowdy, and when we finally settle in after tidying up, I'm exhausted. The fire crackles, warming the lounge. There's gift wrap everywhere, but even in the mess, I've never felt more at ease.

"Can we talk?" I whisper to Tye when everyone is in

conversation.

He nods before taking my hand and leading me into his office. Earlier, we found out so many brutal truths in this room, but that's not what I want to talk about right now.

"What's wrong?" he asks me before I have time to say anything.

Honestly, I'm tired. Exhausted when I think about what has happened over the past few years, so instead of answering, I step closer to Tye. We're inches apart, and for the first time since I can remember, I'm sure of what I want. I stare at his chest, unable to look into his eyes, because I know the moment I do, I'll be lost in them.

"I-I was th-thinking," I mumble, knowing I need to get the words out.

Tye grips my chin gently and tilts my head so I finally meet his questioning gaze. There's a gentleness to him that's always been there. Even now, as strong as he is, his touch is tender.

He leans in until his lips brush against mine. "If this isn't all right, tell me." His words are a warm salve on a wound I knew I had. I never once thought I could be healed, and it will take time. But when his lips find mine, I know I'll everything will be all right.

Heat soothes me when I moan, and I open my mouth to allow his tongue to sweep across mine. It's intimate. I want it. My heart thuds wildly. My stomach flutters like birds taking flight. It's like our first kiss, only softer, more tentative. But, it doesn't lack any of the passion of the first one.

I find confidence when I hear Tye groan, and I wrap my arms around his neck to pull myself closer to him. Our bodies fit together like they were built to slot into place. Like two pieces of the same whole, an image that was torn apart but is now glued back together.

His hands trail over my arms, strong, yet gentle. Then, Tye grips my hips and he pulls me against him, and I can feel how much he wants me. There's no question about it. I don't have a doubt in my mind he's going to finally claim me physically as his.

But then he breaks the kiss. Our breaths are heavy, coming in short spurts. His eyes have darkened, lashes hooded as he regards me. I don't let him go, I can't, not yet. The corner of his mouth tugs into a smirk, one I've come to recognise over the years.

"Ye need to be sure," Tye says in a low, gravelly tone. His voice thick with desire, dark with a promise that, if I say yes, there's no going back. Not anymore, but I don't want to.

"Yes," I whisper. "I'm sure."

His mouth crashes against mine once more, and his hands grip my butt, lifting me against him. We spin around until my back hits the door, and I'm pressed between him and the smooth wooden surface. The thickness of his erection soothes the ache between my thighs when he rolls his hips. I can't stop the moan of bliss that falls from my lips.

"Please," I beg him, looking into those dark eyes. Those orbs filled with need and desire. He wants this as much as I do, and it gives me the confidence to finally voice my needs. "Please, let me forget. Make me forget. I want to think about nothin' else but ye."

"We're leavin'," he says suddenly.

Dropping me to my feet, Tye takes my hand and leads me out to the party. He announces to everyone that we're off, but he doesn't wait for the goodbyes. He practically drags me to his bike.

"We didn't say goodbye," I mumble when he hands me the helmet I wore yesterday when we arrived here.

"Aye," he responds. "They'll understand. It's time I took ye to my home."

I look at him in surprise. "I thought you lived here."

He helps me onto the bike, and I wrap myself around him. I have a feeling he isn't going to be riding slow.

"If ye decide ye want this," Tye says as he glances at me from over his shoulder, "ye'll have to live with me. I won't let ye out of my sight."

I don't have time to reply, because he starts the engine, which rumbles to life, and soon, we're pulling out onto the road that leads us back into Belfast. I hold on tight, and I know that no matter what happens from now on, I'll always have Tye.

CHAPTER NINE

Eirin

Walking into his home feels like coming to a place I longed for. It's as if I had seen it in my dreams time and again, and now, it's a reality. When I was younger, I would imagine what it would be like to have Tye love me, to be with him forever. There wasn't a moment in my life I didn't want to share with him.

He was my best friend.

We shared everything. All those secrets you would usually write in a diary, I told him. But I kept one of the biggest things from him—my feelings. I knew if I told him, he would appease me because he never wanted to see me sad. I didn't want that. Instead, I dreamt of the moment when he would be the one to confess first. Granted, I thought it was a teenage fantasy. A silly thought I put out of my mind. It was only in the dead of night, lying in my bed, when I pondered what it would feel like to have him be my first kiss or my first everything.

And, for the most part, he was.

Now all I'm hoping is that he'll be my last.

There isn't another man for me. Tye is it. He's always been it. Even though all these years have passed, I don't feel nervous.

He leaves me for a short moment, and I wander around the lounge. It's comfortable, with manly colours of brown and grey. What I do notice, though, is that there aren't any soft touches, like cushions or throws. There isn't a woman in his life. I can't stop the smile that pulls at my lips.

He didn't move on. The same as me. That fills me with warmth. He is mine, and I was always meant to be his. Time was stolen from us, and we have a lot of making up to do.

"Come here," he says with a smile, and I turn to find him right behind me.

Gently, he scoops me up into his strong arms, and I've never felt so safe before. He walks us down a hall that leads to his bedroom. Just like the lounge, it's stark. There aren't any photos or any personal touches.

"Do you live here? Or just sleep here?" I ask when he sets me down on my feet.

He looks around, taking in the space as I am. "I've never felt like anywhere was home. Even though the club is basically like family to me, this place has never felt warm."

"Why?" I'm curious. My gaze is focused on his expression. There's a flicker of something there, and when he looks at me, my heart stutters.

"Because I never thought of any one place as home. It was always ye." He steps towards me. "Ye, my sweet girl, have been my home since I first met ye. I just didn't have the balls to tell ye before. And this room was just a place to sleep. I've felt lost for a long time, Einin."

My breath catches in my throat at his sweet words. My pulse is erratic at his confession. I wasn't expecting it. But I find I'm smiling.

"I've had rough days, Tye," I tell him earnestly. "I didn't think I'd make it. Most of the time, I wondered if I'd live through the day or night."

"Ye're safe now." He cups my cheek, a gentle touch that warms me as he skims his thumb over my lips. "And I'm never lettin' ye out of my sight."

And then he leans in and kisses me. His mouth seals over mine, and we become one person, one entity, moving together. Our bodies are moulded to each other.

We fit.

We always have.

The moment the back of my knees hit the mattress, I'm lowered gently onto the bed. It's the first time we've gotten this far. The long ago kiss doesn't even come close to the butterflies currently alive in my belly.

"Ye don't even know just how long I've waited and prayed for this," Tye admits with his gaze locked on mine.

"Really? You prayed?" I tease, which only makes him chuckle as he shakes his head at me. With tentative fingers, he tugs at my top, which slowly slides up my torso and over my head. I can no longer hide the scars from the past. They're all over my flesh, in light raised bumps.

"Tye," I murmur softly when I see the violence on his face. He wants to hurt those who hurt me. It's how he's always been. I don't blame him. I can't be angry, because they will deserve all that's coming to them. "Look at me."

He doesn't meet my stare. Instead, he does something that cracks open my heart and expertly puts it back together again. His lips feather over the raised bumps. The contact making me wince, even though it's a phantom pain, not a physical one.

"You're beautiful," Tye moans as he continues down my body.

When he reaches the waistband of my jeans, he tugs and they come away along with my underwear. I'm in my bra and a pair of socks. But the moment Tye stands, he lifts one of my legs, taking my ankle in his hand, and he pulls the sock off before placing a kiss on the sole of my foot.

He does the same with the other. And then, he drifts his perfectly full lips up my calves to my inner thighs, which sends desire racing up my body. But he doesn't touch me where I want it most. He evades the apex of my thighs and teases his way up to my bra, which he unhooks with ease, and when the material falls away, his eyes turn black with desire.

"Mine." The word is a whisper, but I hear it. "Mine." Each time he repeats it, he kisses me, he sucks my nipples into his mouth, causing an eruption of goosebumps. "Mine." He once again moves down my body, chanting that one word.

Tye has always owned me. He stole my heart from the day we met, and he held it in his hands, safely, for years. I'm lost in the pleasure of his warm breath, his gentle kisses, and his grazing teeth when suddenly, he pushes my thighs apart and he laps at my core, causing my hips to buck in response.

"Tye!" His name is a mewl of need from me, and he does it again. Tasting me. Licking and devouring me. And I can't stop the wetness from coating his tongue.

I've never had anyone do that to me. My body is coiled so tight, I'm sure when I do lose control, I'm going to snap and break. That's what he wants, to break every barrier I have and burrow himself into the shattered pieces. I want that too.

When I glance down, my cheeks heat from embarrassment at Tye between my thighs. In so many ways, he's going to be the first for me. The first man I want to touch me, kiss me, and be inside me. His tongue sends bliss scorching through my veins. A wildfire is lit deep in my core, erupting through every inch of me. My toes curl when he slips two fingers into my pussy, and he curls them to reach a spot that sends me reeling through space.

My head drops back onto the bed, and my eyes shut so tight, I see a galaxy of stars as I cry out his name over and over again. But he doesn't relent. Even as my thighs tremble and my body pulses around his fingers, he continues his ministrations, drawing every drop of release from me.

When Tye finally ceases his torture, and he pulls both digits from my wetness, I open my eyes to see him taste my juices on his fingers. He licks them, savours them as if they were his favourite sweets.

"You're beautiful," he tells me then. "And you're mine. Do you understand that, Einin?" His voice is a raspy vibration. His eyes are black as night. I've never seen him like this.

"Yes," is all I manage to mutter as I slowly sink back to reality.

My gaze doesn't leave Tye as he shoves his jeans, along with his black underwear, down, and I'm met with a strong, beautiful man, no longer the pretty boy who was my best friend. Tye is all grown up.

His cock is hard, jutting out from his hips, and I scoot back on the bed, wondering just how he's going to feel inside me. Silently, he grips himself and strokes a couple of times, and the motion is one of the sexiest things I've ever seen in my life. The muscles on his forearm bulge, and the tip of his erection weeps.

"I want you, my wee bird," he confesses. "I've wanted you for too long."

I watch as he reaches into his bedside table and retrieves a foil wrapper. The sight of him tearing it open and slowly sliding the rubber over his thickness makes my mouth water.

When he's fully sheathed, he looks up at me. The question is shining in his eyes. He wants permission. He needs to know I want this as much as he does. And there is no doubt in my mind.

"Please," I ask him. "I want you to make me forget the past seven years." It's what I wanted when we were back at the club. I thought long and hard about it, and I knew it had to be him. There wasn't a moment in my life I didn't think he would be my first. "Be my last," I whisper, my cheeks hot, and I'm pretty sure they're bright red.

Tye moves over me, holding himself up on his elbows. The tip of his cock nudges the entrance of my pussy, and slowly, as he rolls his hips, he slips inside me. It's a slow, torturous movement as he stretches me open, and I can't stop the hiss of pain from escaping my lips.

"If you want me to stop—"

"No," I say quickly, opening my eyes to find him staring down at me in concern. "Please, Tye. Do it." My words confirm the permission I gave him earlier, and he thrusts in one swift movement.

My back arches as I am filled more than I ever have been, and I can't think of a more perfect way to spend Christmas than connected to the man I love. I stare at Tye, still trying to comprehend this is real. I'm not dreaming. I won't wake in a few minutes and realise I'm not in bed with him but somewhere else.

Twining my hands around his neck, I pull him closer, and when his lips touch mine, I moan. He kisses me while he fucks me. His movements get faster. I'm pinned to the bed, my body open, filled, and dripping wet. The sounds of our bodies moving in sync are accompanied by my whimpers and the rumbling groans of bliss from both of us.

I suck his tongue, tangling it with mine as I lose myself in the moment. Tye reaches for my face, resting his weight on one elbow, and he cups my cheek. Gently, he pulls his lips from mine, breaking the kiss. Those eyes I've come to love, I've come to find solace in, pierce me.

"I love you, Einin," he tells me in a soft whisper that feathers his warm breath over my face. He's perfect in every way. He always has been. And his words of affection grip my heart, filling it.

"I love you too, Tye. I've always loved you," I tell him as he pulls out of me, then sinks his cock in so slowly, I want to cry out and beg him to move faster.

"Feel me," he tells me. "Feel every feckin' inch of my cock," he continues. "It's yours. You're mine. This is the only dick ye'll have inside ye until the day ye feckin' die."

His promise is a balm over my brokenness. It heals me in ways I never expected. And I can't stop the smile from curling on my lips as I look up at him.

"I'll always be yours," I vow.

They're words I don't take lightly. It's a promise I will never break. Because now I've found him, I know I can never let him go.

CHAPTER TEN

Tye

Her body feels like feckin' heaven. Her pussy is warm, wet, and it hugs my dick like it was made for me. I move and I watch as she loses control. With every thrust, Einin moans my name, a song of pleasure I'm givin' her, and I feckin' love it.

I don't stop. I don't slow down, because I can't. Einin feels too good. Her walls tighten around me, pulsin', and as I thrust in deep, her body moulds even closer to mine.

"Please, please, Tye," she begs and I know she needs

to come. Just like I need it.

I reach for her clit and circle it while my mouth captures one of her nipples, and I bite down on it until she's mewlin' for me. The sound is like a drug. My nerves are feckin' sparkin' to life. I need more of her. An addict needin' his fix.

Releasin' her nipple, I lean in close and whisper, "Come fer me." The words are an order, and I pinch the hardened nub between my fingers, causin' her cunt to gush. "Good feckin' girl. Comin' on my dick." I thrust one last time before my orgasm hits me like a feckin' freight train. It sends me over the edge, and I empty myself into the rubber.

I want her raw. Soon enough, we won't be needin' a feckin' condom, because I'm goin'ta make her mine in every way I can. I don't move for a long while, watchin' her face, how her lashes flutter and her plump lips part. Her short breaths come in spurts as she comes down from the high of her orgasm.

When those pretty eyes lock on mine once more, she smiles. The sight of her beauty knocks me feckin' senseless. She's always had this power over me. It's been like that since the moment I first feckin' saw her.

"Thank you," Einin whispers, her eyes glazin' over, and the tears that shimmer on her lashes cause me to panic. "I wanted that for so long. You made me forget. And I love you for it." Her voice cracks.

"I don't want ye to ever fear anything anymore," I tell Einin while I keep my gaze on hers. "Nothin' and nobody will hurt ye again." There's no doubt in my words, because I will kill before I allow anythin' harmful to come near her again.

"My hero." She gifts me a smile, and my heart feckin' stops for a second before poundin' against my ribs.

I move to help her up, then head into the bathroom to discard the condom. When I make my way back into the bedroom, she's lyin' on my bed lookin' like a feckin' seductress if ever I saw one.

Slippin' under the covers, I pull Einin into my arms and I hold her tight. I still can't believe she's here. The reality hasn't yet sunk in, and I know that when I wake in the mornin', she'll still be here. At least, I feckin' hope she will be.

"Will ye tell me what happened?" I ask and I feel her tense in my arms.

She's been through hell, and I don't want to dampen this moment with her, but I need to know. Tomorrow, Monster is goin'ta want ta know more about the men who took her, and I'm goin'ta have ta find the feckers. Once we do, there's no doubt we'll go after them.

Patrick Bragan is still out there. And even though Callia is back, I doubt he'll give up so easily. She told us he said he wanted revenge. For what, I don't feckin' know.

Einin scoots up, liftin' her head to look at me. "I was on the bus travelling to Belfast when it was stopped by five black cars. We didn't know what was happening." The tears I've seen earlier are back, hangin' on her lashes, just waitin' for her to blink. "The other people on the bus were just goin'ta visit family. It wasn't like we had done anything wrong. One of the ol' biddies on the bus was going on about the IRA."

"And ye didn't recognise anyone?"

She shakes her head, and when her eyes close for a second, the tears finally trickle down her cheeks. "Naw, they were strangers to me. I wanted to hide, but there was nowhere to go. The men who got out the cars had guns when they stepped onto the bus. Took me and two other wee girls," she tells me.

"What happened to the other two?"

"Dunno," Einin says. "Never saw them again after we got to the private airport." She drops her gaze to my chest. Her focus must be blurry now because the tears are streamin' down her face. I reach up to swipe at them, but more tumble down. It's as if the dam has broken. She needs this. "I was taken across the pond, but I wasn't there fer very long."

"Can you remember any of the faces of the men?"

"Aye," she says with a nod. "If I see them again, I'll definitely know them."

This is good because I can pull up files from the databases from all law enforcement agencies. If we can get names, we can find them. No doubt it won't only be us lookin'. Scotland Yard, The Garda, and MI5 will all be interested in the information we can pick out.

"Tomorrow," I start slowly, hopin' to keep her calm. "I want to try somethin' if ye're up to it."

Einin glances at me with a watery stare. "What is it?"

"If I can get ye the photos of these feckers, will ye be able to tell me who they are?"

"Yes," she confirms, her voice stronger. "The sooner we find them, the quicker they'll pay for what they've done."

I always knew she was a strong wee bird. Her wings may have been clipped, but it's not broken her spirit. I know she's been hurt. There's no doubt about it. But she's a fighter.

"Then that's what we'll do," I tell her. "But fer now, we need to sleep."

We nestle into each other. Einin fits in my arms. She's a piece of me I had fer so long, and when it was taken away, I wasn't myself.

When I told her earlier I never felt at home without her, I meant it. She was always the place I would want to come to after a long day. If somethin' had hurt me, if I was angry at anyone, it was always Einin who could calm me down, who could bring me back down to earth.

I won't lose her again.

∞

The sun streams through the windows. I forgot to close the feckin' blinds last night. The only thing I could think of was holdin' onto my girl. But when I open my eyes, I don't see her beside me. Panic washes over me like ice water.

Shovin' the blankets off, I push to my feet and race to the bathroom to find it empty. But when I walk into the kitchen, my erratic feckin' pulse eases up.

She's standin' at the kitchen counter wearin' nothin' but a pair of her knickers and one of my T-shirts. She doesn't hear me enter the room, her focus on whatever the feck she's got on the stove. The smell of something delicious hits my nostrils and I smile at the thought of her bein' my wife, cookin' breakfast together before we head to the club and work.

It's a fantasy I've had before. But when I thought she just didn't want me, I buried it deep down because I couldn't come to terms with the hurt it caused. The idea of not bein' with her was too much to handle. It was easier to ignore it than to face it.

Perhaps that's why now I'm still in awe of her bein' here. When she spins around, her eyes widen in surprise. Her mouth pops open, and I'm lost in thoughts of what I'd like to do to her right here in the kitchen.

"Enjoyin' yerself?" I ask, leanin' against the doorframe with my arms folded.

Her cheeks darken from pink to a shade of red. "Yes," she says. "Made some breakfast. Wasn't much in your fridge."

"I don't eat here often."

Einin looks up at me. The sadness in her eyes at my statement grips my heart. She can tell I wasn't happy here. I was livin' my life, but there wasn't a place I truly felt at peace.

The club is good for me. It gives me the focus I need when things get too much, but that soul-deep happiness was always out of reach. I knew it was because I could never have the love I'd lost. I could never have Einin.

"I'm sorry." Her whisper is filled with anguish, which forces me to go to her.

I stop inches from her, and I cup her cheeks in my hands. Her gaze lasers in on mine. She can't look away.

"Ye're here now," I assure her before pressin' a kiss to her lips then I step back. "What's for brekkie then?"

"Nothin' special," she tells me before turning back to whatever she's been busy with. "I am not a great cook." While Einin is busyin' herself, I step up behind her and slide my arms around her waist. My chin rests on her shoulder and I press a kiss to her neck.

"Anythin' ye do will be grand," I whisper. "Today, we have a lot of work to do."

I release her and let her finish up while I sit at the counter. When she places a plate in front of me, I'm astounded. Even though it's fairly basic eggs, toast, and some bacon—there are spices on the top I didn't know I had in the cupboard.

"Like I said, nothing special." She sets down a mug of freshly brewed coffee, which I always have in the house, before joinin' me. "Tell me what you do?" she asks before bitin' into the toast.

"Well," I say, lookin' up to find her starin' at me. "The club needs someone who can hack into systems and gather information. After ye left Ballycastle, I finished off my final year at school and headed down to Belfast. Da paid fer me to come here. Sold the shop."

"He sold the shop?" Her mouth pops open. Surprise clear on her face. She knows how much that place meant to my da.

"Aye." I nod. "He said he didn't want me to end up like him, stuck there with no future." I consider this for a moment before I say, "We should head up the road and see the town. I can take ye to see ye ma's grave."

"I'd like that." Einin's sadness is bone-deep.

I can't imagine losin' Da and not knowin', and then when I finally find out, realisin' I'll never get to say goodbye. The old man is gettin' old now. I have to get up there and see how he's doin'. And I'm sure it will be nice for Einin to be back.

"We need to finish up some shite at the club, and then soon, we're takin' a few days off."

I don't think he'll mind. I've been workin' every day for months, and I need the time to clear my head. There's somethin' I want to do up in my old home town as well, and I need Einin with me.

Suddenly, Einin asks, "Would you teach me to do what you do?" She waves her hand in the air. "For work I mean."

"Ye want ta get into computers?"

"Yes, I think it will allow me to help other girls who've gone through what I have. And maybe even save a few who've been taken and sold off like livestock."

I can hear the anger in her voice. It's twisted around every word. I don't blame her, to be fair. Over the years of me workin' at the club, diggin' into law enforcement databases, I've found so many cases of missin' persons. Girls of every age, some even younger than I ever thought possible. I vowed I would spend my life catchin' the bastards who do this shite, and I'm thankful I'm able to. It's the reason I offered my services to the club. Monster's focus on the criminal organisations is as strong as mine. Now that we know Bragan is behind the traffickin', we can knuckle down and find the fecker.

"Then ye'll work with me," I tell Finin. If she thinks she can handle it, I'm not goin'ta deny her the opportunity to get her revenge. This way, I can keep her safe in the office while she feels as if she's doin' somethin'. 'Cause there ain't a chance in hell I'm lettin' her walk out into the line of fire.

"Let's get ready then," she announces before finishin' up her breakfast and sashayin' her sweet arse through my flat. When I hear the shower turn on, I follow close behind because I'm in need of another taste of my wee bird.

CHAPTER ELEVEN

Einin

Even though Tye agreed to teach me, I'm not sure I have a place at the club. When we walk in, I'm greeted with smiles and hugs, but I'm still a stranger. They don't know me, and I've learnt over the years, people can smile, they can be friendly, but it doesn't mean they like you.

Tye is the only person I'm connected to, and if he were to tell me to leave, I wouldn't have a choice. At least I'm free. I could go back to Ballycastle and work in one of the few restaurants as a waitress or something similar. But it's not where my heart lies. And those thoughts are plaguing me as we enter Tye's office.

He pulls up a chair, which he sets beside his, and he gestures for me to sit. Once we're situated, he turns on the multiple screens, and all I see are lines of numbers and text. It's going to be a challenge to learn, but I know Tye will be able to show me the ropes. All I need is to focus.

"Are ye sure ye want ta do this? We can wait a few days," Tye says when he glances at me over his shoulder.

Shaking my head, I meet his questioning stare. "Yes, I'm sure. The sooner we get started, the better." I've made my decision, and I can't go back on it. I don't want to. This is going to help me heal. "I want to get this started. The new year is almost here, and I'm ready to start fresh. I've been given a second chance. I won't waste it."

A small smile plays on his lips. He knows I'm stubborn. I always have been, ever since I was a little one. Nothing has changed. And Tye knows better than to argue with me.

"Right then," he says as he gets started with the explanations of what he's doing.

The passion in his voice when he talks about his work is astounding. He's always been good with tech, even when we were at school. But seeing him now, it's as if he was made to sit here and do good with a few key strokes at a time.

After a couple of hours, I'm starting to fidget. There are so many names on the screen, so many missing girls, it breaks my heart. I was one of those. And all I can do is pray we find as many of them as we can, if not all. It's a large undertaking, and it's not going to happen overnight. But if we can make a dent in the enormous list, I'll hopefully be able to feel less guilty for being freed.

"What about this?" I ask, pointing at a folder I noticed on the desktop, but didn't want to pry. However, my curious nature has gotten the best of me.

Tye glances at me, something flickering in his eyes. "It's..."

He turns back to the screen, and he clicks on the folder. When it opens, my heart catapults into my chest. Looking back at me is a photo of myself and Tye when I was sixteen. He's only a year older than me, but in the picture, he is a young man while I still look like a girl.

We're both smiling, and the fair is in full swing in the background. There are a few mates I now recall from school laughing and hugging in the photo as well.

But it's the image of me and Tye that's gripped my heart.

"I haven't seen that in so long," I whisper as the tears burn my eyes. "I remember that day like it was yesterday." Only because it was the day I realised how much I loved Tye.

He'd bought me some fudge, while we played football on the pitch not far from the centre of town. I'd scraped my knee, and he crouched down to make sure I wasn't bleeding too badly. He patched me up without question, but it was his fingertips that caused the sensations to warm my cheeks. There were goosebumps all over me. It was a spark that never stopped.

"It kept me company while I worked," Tye admits before he turns his chair towards me. "There's somethin' I wanted to ask ye," he says slowly.

My heart leaps into my throat, and I can't find the words to respond to him. All I can do is look at him silently as he stares right back at me.

"I want you to stay," he finally says and the breath I'd been holding is whooshed from my lungs in a long exhale. "I mean, ye don't have ta stay with me, but ye belong here. This family is made up of people from broken pasts. They all have a story to tell, so if ye were worried about fittin' in, ye'll belong, just like I do."

For a long, heavy moment, all I can do is stare at him. I didn't consider he'd want me here.Yes, we'd slept together last night, but that was something that had been in the cards for years. I had wanted to give him my virginity.

When I don't immediately respond, Tye says, "Ye don't have to be with me if ye don't want te."

"Are you even listening to the shite you're spewing? You're having a laugh. Aren't ye?" I giggle when he glares at me. "I've wanted to be with you since I was sixteen," I admit. "Do you think I'm going to *not* want you?"

"I didn't want ta assume," he throws back, but the smile on his face causes my chest to fill with emotion I wasn't expecting.

"I'll stay," I tell him, and he quickly pulls me onto his lap.

"Promise me ye'll never leave me again," Tye whispers along my lips. The warmth of him causes me to blush as his hands trail down my back. His touch is electric. It always has been.

"You know I won't."

"I just didn't want ye to feel as if ye needed to be with me. I never want you to feel obligated by anythin'

I ask of ye."

I'm sure he's worried about what I've been through. And I want to talk to someone about it, to work through the past, but Tye is my world. He always has been.

"I know." I twine my hands around his neck. "But I'm here to stay. So, you've no need to worry about me walking out ever again. I'm making my own choices from now on."

The smile that curls his lips is perfect. It's one of the reasons I would spend all my time staring at him. When Tye smiles, it's as if the sun is streaming from within him.

"I have a present fer ye," he tells me. "I was goin'ta give it to ye yesterday, but with everythin' that went on, I wanted to wait until we had time to ourselves."

"I didn't get you anything." Even though I know he won't care about it, I feel as if I'd like to get him something.

"Ye're gift enough fer me, Einin." He reaches for a drawer in his desk and pulls it open. Inside is a mess of stationery, but amongst everything, is a small box that he sets on my palm. "It was somethin' I got fer ye before ye left. I just didn't have the bollocks to give it to ye."

I look up at him with the box in my hand. My pulse is thrumming in my ears, and my throat is thick with emotion. We used to buy each other presents every year. Twice a year—birthdays and Christmas.

I lower my gaze before opening the box, and my eyes fill with tears when I see the pretty ring shimmerin' at me. The stone is beautiful, with colours that remind me of an ocean.

"This is beautiful, Tye," I whisper past the lump in my throat. Swallowing back my emotions, I fight the tears that threaten to fall. I didn't expect something like this, least of all when I've just got him back. "You know finding you again was gift enough for me."

He chuckles, causing me to look up. "Aye? Want me to return it then?"

"Naw." Giggling, I swat him on the chest. "I just didn't expect this."

"It's a promise," he tells me. "I want ye to know that no matter what happens from here till my final breath, I'm not leavin' you alone. Ever."

"Stalker," I tease before pressing my lips to his.

"I think ye'd like me to stalk yer sexy arse," Tye growls against my lips then he deepens the kiss. Warmth floods me in that moment. I smile against his mouth. Suddenly, he breaks contact and reaches for the ring. "Time to slip this on. And if ye take it off, I'll spank yer wee arse."

It fits perfectly on the ring finger on my right hand. My left hand will have to wait for the day we make this permanent. But for now, I couldn't be happier. Everything seems to be working out.

"I'm happy," I tell him, looking deep into his eyes.

"I know things are goin' to work out," Tye tells me, a smile creasing the corners of his eyes, as his lips curl upwards. "And I know ye're goin'ta need time to work through the past few years."

"But I have you," I whisper. "The only thing that got me through the worst moments was thinking about you. Even though I was convinced you'd moved on, I remembered our friendship. I remembered the kiss." My admission is a soft murmur, but I know he heard me.

I never told him then what it felt like kissing him. I was so convinced he only did it because I was leaving, I kept all those feelings bottled up, hidden away from him, because I didn't want to lose my best friend.

"Nothin' will ever take ye away from me again," Tye confirms before he wraps his arms around me. They're strong, warm, and I nestle against his chest.

"I didn't think I belonged here," I whisper into his

neck as I hide from what I can only imagine is a glare. "When I first walked in, I was the outsider, and it was as if you'd got a new family. I didn't want to be the hanger on. You know?"

Tye releases me and cups my cheeks, forcing me to look at him. I can't move away. My gaze lands on his and I'm held hostage by the fire burning in his eyes.

"Ye belong with me," he tells me. "And if that means we stay here, then so be it. If we have to leave one day, then we do it together."

"Sounds like a deal," I say before pressing my lips to his.

"Are ye workin' or fuckin'?" Monster's deep voice startles us both, and we turn to find him on the threshold of the office. He's grinning as he leans against the doorframe to regard us, arms folded across his chest. He looks like a da who's caught his teen daughter with the boy next door.

"Aye," Tye says. "Just takin' a wee break."

"Get on with it," Monster replies as he enters the room, completely unperturbed by the sight before him. "Spoken to Venier. He says there's been some movement at the pier. I think we need to make a run to the docks tonight. I want to go when it's dark."

"Sounds good. I'll trace any comms on shipments

comin' in. I haven't seen any so far, but if Bragan is makin' a move, I'll find it."

I move off Tye's lap and settle in the chair beside him. He gets to work quickly. Watching him in his element is intriguing. He loves what he does, and it shows because his focus is on the screen.

"Ye stayin' with us?" Monster asks, looking directly at me.

"Yes, if you'll have me."

He narrows his gaze, and for a moment, I'm pretty sure he's about to refuse me, but then he grins. "Can't have one of my best lads leavin' me now." He gestures with his chin towards Tye, and it makes me smile. "Ye're welcome to the family. We'll have a party this weekend to initiate ye."

"I wanted to take her up to Ballycastle as well," Tye says, leaning back in his chair. "Just a couple of days."

"Aye." Monster nods. "Take as much time as ye need. Just know if we find Bragan, we're movin' in. I won't wait this time. I want the fecker dead."

"Grand, I'll keep track of everythin' on my laptop anyways. If somethin' comes up, we'll know about it."

"No bother." Monster pushes to his feet. "Get me somethin' within the hour. I want to call church and have everyone on the same page about tonight."

Once he's gone, Tye and I get to work. We need to find the bastard, and we need to find him quickly.

For the first time in a long while, I'm excited about what's to come. I have a future, and I'm not walking away from it now.

CHAPTER TWELVE

Tye

From the moment we cross into Ballycastle, everythin' feels different. The city is far behind us, while the small town we both grew up in sits before us. The silence is overwhelmin', and fer a moment, I'm convinced we've made a mistake comin' home.

The thought hits me. Home. The only time I have ever considered this town home was when she was here. Einin was the one I looked to when I thought of that word. Havin' her back has been a godsend, even though I've given up prayin' a long while ago.

Tonight the club ride out to the docks, but Monster insisted I leave. He wanted me and Einin to work on trackin' Bragan while we were up here. He knows what it means to find love, to capture it and hold it in your hands, and never want to let go.

Einin is new to this life, and puttin' her in danger wasn't an option. Also, we are more useful behind the screens than in a fight. We can see who's comin' and what's goin'ta happen before it does. I've got surveillance on the whole pier, and whatever happens, I'll know if the brothers are in danger before they even leave the clubhouse.

I pull up to the graveyard. It's not changed since the last time I walked around, lookin' at familiar names. Growin' up in such a small town, you know everyone's shite. From who's havin' an affair, to who hates who.

Einin holds on to my shoulders as she swings her leg over my bike. Havin' her behind me was distractin', and I'm pretty sure her roamin' hands felt exactly what she does to me.

"It still looks how I remember," Einin whispers when we're standing in front of the two heavy metal gates. The entrance has never been locked. I'm not sure why they even have gates. Is it to keep people out or keep them in?

I take her hand and lead her into the grounds. The grey headstones peek at us from the ground. Rows of them, and I'm sure more are added all the time. When we reach Einin's ma's stone, we stop.

I release her hand from mine and allow her a moment of silence. She missed the funeral. She didn't even know her ma had died. Anger once again slithers over me. I wanted nothin' more than to keep Einin safe and I failed her.

Monster understands the rage I feel. When I spoke to him the day before we found her, he gave me advice and calmed me down, but each time I think about it, I can't help but feel as if I want to kill.

There's a long road ahead of us. I know this. For Einin, it's going to take months, maybe years to heal from the past. She drops to her knees and places her hands on her thighs. Her shoulders shake as she looks at her ma's name engraved on the slab of granite.

I crouch behind her and place my hands on her shoulders. In the silence of the kirk yard, she cries. Crows squawk overhead, remindin' me of the times I would watch them shimmer in the sun. Their ink black wings glintin' in the daylight.

"Do you think she was in pain?" Einin asks me suddenly, bringin' me back to her. She glances at me over her shoulder, and the pain in her eyes tightens my chest.

"I'm not sure, darlin'. I don't think so. Maybe we can chat to my da and see if he knows anythin'." Knowin' him, he would have checked in on her ma, which means he can give Einin more insight than I can.

Einin nods, then turns back to the grave. I push to my feet and take a step back, allowin' her to say what she needs. Death comes to us all. It's inevitable, and those who are left behind are the ones who need to come to terms with it. Speakin' to the dead is somethin' I've only ever done a handful of times.

When my ma passed on, I hated the world. She was the first and only person to teach me to be soft, as well as strong. Her words replay in my mind so clearly, "*Ye treat those who deserve it with love, affection, but ye can also stand up fer yerself. It saves you from bein' taken advantage of through yer life.*"

She taught me that violence is a choice. I may be a lad, but respondin' with ye fists isn't always an answer. And I've always lived that way, but the man who took Einin, deserves what's comin' to him.

"We can go now," Einin says as she stops beside me. "Thank you for bringing me here." Her smile lights up her face, and her teary stare is a punch to the gut.

"Ye sure?"

"Yes." She nods before takin' my hand. "I've said what I needed to."

We head back to the bike, and once the engine rumbles to life, I pull onto the road that leads up to Da's place. I no longer consider it mine. After I left, I put it behind me. He was more in love with the wee cottage than I was. It overlooks the ocean, which is the only thing it's got goin' fer it.

Pullin' up to the place I grew up in, I turn off the engine and take Einin's hand before makin' my way up the short path that leads to the front entrance. Before I can knock, Da opens the door. He still looks good for his age.

"Now what do we have 'ere?" A smile cracks on his face when he glances behind me and sees Einin. "Ye've grown into a beauty, wee one. Come inside. Let me look at ye."

He takes her hands and brings them to his face. An affectionate kiss on her knuckles makes her smile. My da always loved Einin as if she were his kin.

"It's nice to see you again."

"Aye, and ye've brought my lad back," Da tells her with a chuckle.

I shut the door behind me just before Da surprises

me and pulls me into a hug. He's never been overly affectionate with me. I wonder if old age has finally hit him and now he wants those lost moments.

"It's good to see ye, Son."

"Aye," I reply. "It's good to be back. I wanted Einin to see her ma's grave."

I know there's some explainin' we'll need to do. He'll want to know why she didn't come home fer her ma's funeral. But fer now, we settle in the lounge while he insists on makin' us drinks.

Coffee fer me, hot chocolate fer Einin.

The house hasn't changed. It's as if I've walked back in time. Da joins us and settles himself in the large armchair he used to favour when I was a kid.

"Ye ma's passin' was a sad one in the town," he tells Einin. "She always spoke of ye, told us ye were so busy."

"Well... Something happened when I left. I was on my way to school when the bus was hijacked. I was taken."

Da's face falls, and he turns ashen at the news. "What?"

"Yes. I was held captive for seven years," Einin explains, but she doesn't go into too much detail. "But then, a day before Christmas, Tye found me."

Da's questionin' gaze falls on me. "Ye found her?"

Noddin', I say," Aye, there's some shite goin' down with the mob."

"Ye gettin' involved in all this now?" His brows furrow, and I know it's out of concern rather than a tellin' off.

"I need to help these girls, Da," I insist. "I'm doin' somethin' good. Isn't that what ye wanted?"

"Aye, but I don't need my boy gettin' killed. Ye hear me."

"I won't," I promise, but it's difficult to assure him. He, of all people, knows it's not easy when you've committed to somethin'. Da was in the army for years after he'd turned eighteen. He's been on the front line, seen shite go down that no human being should.

"I just want yers both safe." The concern in his voice is evident.

"We will be," I tell him, and that's the end of that conversation.

One thing about Da, he never lingers on anythin' fer too long. It's one of the reasons I always found it easy to talk to him. He'd offer his advice, and that would be the end of it.

EPILOGUE

Einin

Happiness is no longer a fantasy or a fleeting moment. It's my life. The rain has cleared up for the time being, and I wonder if we'll have some sunshine this weekend for the celebrations.

The club wanted to do something fun, and when we suggested a St. Patrick's Day party, everyone was on board. The months of darkness have passed. Even though the threat of the mob boss returning to Belfast is still hanging over our heads, there is a sense of calm.

We all know he'll be back. But for now, we're

focusing on the present day. Tye has tracking software running to make sure we know the moment Patrick Bragan lands in the country. If he's here, we will know. Even the peelers are working with us to make sure he's arrested.

Opening the curtains, I watch the city hustle by. When Tye asked me to move in with him, I couldn't refuse. We have known each other for most of our lives, and there isn't a day that goes by when I don't want to be near him. Even though it's been a few months since he saved me, there are times I'm still anxious, nervous to go out alone.

Therapy has helped, and being with the club has given me a sense of family. My heart still hurts that I lost my ma and I couldn't be there to say goodbye to her. That kind of sadness will never go away, but slowly, I'll learn to live with the ache in my chest. She was good to me. She never stopped loving me. Even when I became a bratty teen, she would always offer advice.

Now that she's gone, I miss it. I swipe at the lone tear that trickles down my cheek, and I smile. If it weren't for her, I wouldn't be here, and I plan to make the most of the life I've been given. To honour her memory, we plan to head back to Ballycastle soon and clear out the house and turn it into a safe haven for girls we manage to free from trafficking.

Tye is supporting my efforts, and with his expertise, we'll be able to find girls and women who go missing. Now that he's focused on the task, the rest of the brothers have stepped up and said they'll do anything they can to help.

The peelers now see us as partners to bring in the criminals. They know we have our hands in a few different businesses, including our connection with the Italians.

Monster is a good man.

And so are the rest of the brothers.

"My girl ready to go?" Tye walks into the bedroom freshly showered. He's still dripping wet with a towel wrapped around his hips.

Every inch of this man is sculpted to perfection. I doubt I'll ever tire of looking at him because he truly is breath taking.

"Yes." I turn to face him fully.

"Enjoyin' the view?" He arches a brow at me before whipping the towel off. The thickness of his cock has me salivating to taste, to savour him, but we're going to be late.

"I am, but you know we need to be there before—"

He ignores my protests and rushes for me. A squeal breaks free from my lips as I turn and run. We're on either side of the bed, and I know, he'll catch me. I race for the door, but Tye is too quick. His arms wrap around my middle, and he lifts me off my feet. Seconds later, I'm bouncing on the mattress.

Tye moves onto the bed and hovers over me. His lips capture mine, and he kisses me deeply. Each time he touches me, every time he kisses me, it's as if there's an electric current shooting through me. I feel alive. Sparked by my need and desire for him and his passion and love for me.

My tongue sweeps along his before I suck it gently into my mouth, causing him to groan against my lips. Dips and peaks of his chiselled torso press against me, holding me hostage. But I'm not longer a captive. I'm a willing prisoner to him.

"Please," I beg shamelessly. I can't stop myself, because when his hips roll, his cock rubs against my core, sending a delicious thrill of want through me. "Please, Tye."

"My sweet, needy wee bird," he coos against my lips.

I watch as he moves back to tug off his tee, then the clank of his belt buckle echoes in the room. He's beautiful to look at. Naked or clothed. But right now,

I want him completely and utterly naked to my touch.

He pulls at my leggings, taking my knickers along with them. I discard my top, and soon enough, we're skin on skin with the tip of his cock at my entrance.

"Ready for me?" he asks with a smirk curling his perfectly full lips. The dark pink of his tongue darts out to lick at my lips, and I lift my hips to nudge him inside me. A chuckle vibrates in his chest. "So feckin' needy for me," he says. "I love it."

He doesn't need more urging, because he thrusts into my pussy, fully-seated, filling me up and stealing my breath. Tye's mouth trails over my cheek, down to my neck, and he sucks the sensitive flesh into his mouth. His teeth graze against me, causing another whimper to escape. My nipples against his chest send sparks to every inch of my body.

"Feck," Tye growls when I wrap my legs around his waist and I pull him in deeper.

Needing him to give me more, I scrape my nails down his back, digging in as I feel myself get closer to the edge. With every deep thrust of his cock, he slams inside me, and when he pulls out, he rubs against the spot that has fireworks going off behind my eyelids.

"Yes, please, please," I beg, chant. I don't know what I need, but when he captures one of my nipples in his mouth and bites down gently, I pulse around him.

"That's it, sweet girl," he coaxes before mimicking the action on my other nipple. His teeth bite, then his tongue soothes. The pain and pleasure has me soaring into the abyss of euphoria. His hand gently grips my throat, and he pulls away to look me in the eye. "Come for me." His command has me teetering.

"Only for you," I promise when he tightens his hold.

I finally fall. And my body convulses while my eyes roll back. Bliss. White sparks. I shake and tremble underneath him as he thrusts so deep, it feels as if he's trying to touch my very fucking soul.

The warmth of his release floods me, filling me, and his mouth steals a kiss, gentle, soft, and affectionate. His hand is on my face, cupping it, and when I open my eyes once more, I find love shimmering in his eyes.

"Ye're mine," he tells me. "I'll always be yer last."

I nod. I can't find words to respond, so all I can do is move my head up and down. I never thought I would be here. There were times in the years I was gone when I was convinced I was going to die. I welcomed it at times. But Tye found me again. He took what was his all along, my heart and soul.

Now I can have my happily ever after with a family I

didn't see coming and a man I always knew owned me, heart and soul.

THE END

Sneak Peek

MONSTER

PROLOGUE

Monster

10 years ago

I was brought up a religious Catholic boy. My ma made sure I went to church every Sunday and said my prayers every night. Even though I was convinced talking to a man I couldn't see was stupid, she would slap me about the head and tell me to do it anyway. Her influence on my life is the reason I'm here today, alive and not lying beside my da six feet under. She needed me just as much as I needed her. At twenty-eight, I still live with her, wanting to show her that no matter what, I'll be by her side.

I obeyed the rules she set out for me when I was growin' up. Made sure I didn't get myself into trouble, at least for a while. It wasn't until I hit sixteen and got into life with the motorcycle club that it all went south. Which brings me to today. The whispers I'll be takin' over from Da have been nonstop over the past couple weeks, and I'm pretty sure Ma has been dreading this day since she had me.

The thing is, I tried. I truly did. I wanted to be the son my ma could be proud of, and even though I've done some stupid shite, I still know right from wrong. I watched Da fuck up too many times to count, and I vowed to never be like him.

You can't stay innocent forever. Not when you live in Belfast. Northern Ireland has always been famous for the shite that goes down on the daily. It's as if the world is watching, waiting for another storm to hit. Violence was a way of life, not something to be feared.

And when I was a youngen, I didn't think about how much my life would change when I was old enough to be dragged into the darkness with my da. It wasn't the usual worries that bothered me, it was the danger that arrived with coming of age. That's what Da called it at the time. I knew I would need to step up and take over.

There was no doubt in my mind I had a duty to the club. But I convinced myself it would be when I turned eighteen, and not before that.

My da was a leader.

He had men who followed him into the flames, and they all came out on the other side. Walking around like they owned the world, even though the country was burning around them. Unscathed by what life threw at them, ignorant to the people who needed their help. The problem was, they became overconfident.

When you don't know loss, pain, or heartache, you think you are invincible.

They did.

My da convinced his men they would live forever. But that didn't happen, and he left me and Ma on our own. The memory of the war he started is still fresh in my mind. Only two years have passed since he died, and I notice how Ma still seems as if she's walkin' around in a trance.

I lift my stare to her, hoping she'll look at me, but she doesn't. As I sip my coffee, I wonder when she'll stop missin' him, if ever. She may be gettin' older, but she's still the strong woman I've always known her to be. It's Sunday; she's dressed in her favourite outfit as she gets ready to go to church. I may not be joinin' her, but she'll pray for me. It's what she tells me every week.

"I'll pray for you," her words come as she grabs her purse and glances my way. She still loves me, has hope for me, even though I may not believe in what she does. I don't go to church or pray. I gave up on that a long time ago. But the way my ma looks at me is nothin' short of a miracle—her expression filled with love, with affection she shouldn't feel. But she does. One thing about her is she's stubborn. Must be where I get it from.

"Aye." I chuckle. "No need. You know I'm goin' straight to hell," I tell her. It's somethin' I believe with every fibre of my being. When I was thirteen, I remember standin' and singing some feckin' hymn that meant nothin' to me. It was part of the service, but when I looked up, my gaze caught the priest's, and he smirked. It was as if he knew I was tainted, and he made the sign of the cross.

Ma used to call me her wee monster. I was a nightmare growing up, and even now, as an adult, the name stuck. Which is why it's my road name. I've come into my own, and I'm proud of it.

She tuts at me. "Ach, don't you go talkin' like that now." She leans up onto her tiptoes to press a kiss to my cheek. "He knew what was comin'," Ma says in a soft voice. "You just make sure to walk through that door safe tonight," she tells me before she steps out into the early morning sunshine. It's a beautiful day. You'd never think I'm about to step into my father's shoes. I didn't want it. I was happy being the Vice President of the club, but it's the line of succession. There's too much to do without fighting what's inevitable.

Once I'm alone in the house, I wonder if I'll ever see the disdain on Ma's face when I become President. It's not a life she wanted for me, but there is no choice. I can't walk away from a legacy. Her words ring in my ears. It's somethin' she's always said to me before walkin' out of the house.

Makin' my way to the small office I set up after Da died, I shut the door, and I settle in behind the desk. We have a meetin' later, and I have ta get my shite in order. Opening the clubs on the Main Street this weekend has been grand. But we need more income. There's only one way I can see to get that, but I'm not prepared to deal drugs. Weapons, maybe. I'm about to call my VP, Rebel, when gunshots ring through the air.

Panic twists in my gut because I realise I didn't hear the engine on Ma's car startin'. Crouching down, I creep to the office door and down the hallway before another round of gunfire hits the windows of our home. The place I grew up in. Even though I have the clubhouse and all that comes with it, farmland that spans hundreds of acres just outside Belfast, I've always stayed home. Being in the city energises me.

When I reach the living room, I pull my gun from the leather holster and get to my knees. I can't take any chances when it comes to violence, when it comes to being under attack. I'm alone here, and if someone did want to get in, I can only fight so much. Being outnumbered has never bothered me, not even now, but the thought of Ma being out there alone, it's got me pushing to my feet. I lean against the wall beside our front door and breathe in deeply.

Listening for any more noise outside, I close my eyes and focus. I wait a couple of minutes before I pull open the front door, hiding behind the wooden surface, and show my gun first. Silence greets me when I do, which means they're gone, or they're waitin' on me to walk out.

But when no shots come, I step out into the line of fire with my heart beating a rhythm against my chest. My ribs ache from the thrum, and as I make my way onto the small porch where Ma and Da used to sit every evening, I take in the destruction in front of me.

In death there is silence.

It's only when I reach the wee garden, do I see it. Blood. I've never seen so much mayhem in one small area before. Droppin' my gun, I race out into the street, forgetting there are men out here who want me dead. I find my mother's car still in the same place she parked it yesterday, with holes all through the doors, the one side completely fuckin' obliterated.

It's not that which has me fallin' to my knees, though, it's the ol' lady in the driver's seat. She's not breathing. The window has shattered, glass everywhere, and her mouth hangs open while her eyes are wide with shock as she stares out into the abyss.

Pain shatters me. The twisting in my gut only tightens when I reach for her neck and place two fingers against it. The wrinkled flesh against my fingertips doesn't do anything because there's no heartbeat. Her breath doesn't come. There isn't a final gasp or a last word.

"Ma," I call to her, but it's in vain because I know she won't answer. She'll never answer me again. There'll never be another prayer sent to heaven for me. Not that I believe in it, but she offered a comfort when she said it. All her life she prayed for me. She wanted what was best for me. The woman stood by me when she learned I would become President of the Royal Bastards. She didn't tell me to leave. Ma loved me unconditionally, as I did her.

Love comes with a price.

I pull open the door, and my mother's body slumps toward me. Catching her, I blink away the tears that threaten. They burn, and I want nothing more than to give my life for hers. The bastards were after me. Whoever they were, they wanted me dead, but instead, they stole the last good thing in my life.

The image of her blurs, and my vision is stolen when I drop my head against hers and shut my eyes. And I do the one thing I haven't done in years–I pray. Never once did I think I'd be on my knees, calling out to a God who long ago had forsaken me, beggin' for him to bring my mother to life. She always wanted me to join her in prayer. And it's in her death I finally do.

I don't know how long I'm on my knees, but when I feel a hand on my shoulder, I glance up, the sun momentarily blinding me. He steps into the light, and I see Rebel staring down at me. The look on his face tells me everything I need to know.

Today I become the President.

And today, I make a vow of revenge.

If you haven't yet met Monster, head over to Amazon to grab book one in the series now!

https://books2read.com/ABM-RBMC1

Ready to spend Paddy's Day with the Royal Bastards? Head to Amazon to make sure Lucky Clover lands on your Kindle!

https://books2read.com/LC-OneClick

ALSO BY DANI RENÉ

Head to my website here for a full list of my incredible titles

www.danirene.com

ABOUT THE AUTHOR

Dani is a *USA Today* Bestselling Author of seductive and deviant romance.

Her books range from the dark to emotional, but every hero is alpha, and each heroine is strong-willed, bringing the men down to their knees.

She now lives in the UK, after moving from Cape Town, exploring cemeteries and old buildings while plotting her next book.

When she's not writing, she can be found binge-watching the latest TV series, or working on graphic design. She has a healthy addiction to reading, tattoos, coffee, and ice cream.

www.danirene.com | info@danirene.com

Find me at @danireneauthor on

Facebook | Instagram | Pinterest | TikTok | Spotify